FILTHY GODS

FALLING FOR CATASTROPHE

USA TODAY BESTSELLING AUTHOR

MICHELLE HERCULES

FALLING FOR CATASTROPHE

A FILTHY GODS NOVEL

MICHELLE HERCULES

INFINITE SKY PUBLISHING

Paperback ISBN: 978-1-950991-98-3

PLAYLIST

GOODBYE AGONY - Black Veil Brides
DEATHWISH - Red Sun Rising
TEETH - 5 Seconds of Summer
THIS HIGH - The Man Who
OPEN YOUR EYES - Snow Patrol
WOLVES - Selena Gomez
WALLS COULD TALK - Halsey
INFERNO - Sub Urban, Bella Poarch
CHASING HIGHS - Too Close To Touch
SEVEN NATION ARMY - The White Stripes
SHAMELESS - Camila Cabello
REVENGE - P!nk & Eminem
TOO LOST IN YOU - Sugababes
LOVE AGAIN - Dua Lipa, GARABATTO
SURRENDER - Angels & Airwaves
BAD AT LOVE - Halsey
OVERTURE - Black Veil Brides
STORM - Antonio Vivaldi, Vanessa-Mae

PROLOGUE

NICOLA / ISABELLE

Run, run, don't stop, don't look back, just run, run. The mantra keeps me going. I stumble over an exposed tree root and fall hard on my hands and knees, but I don't even register the pain. I get up and keep running while my heart feels like it's going to explode out of my chest.

The forest is quiet tonight; there's no sound of animals, as if they sense evil is on the prowl, hunting me. Even the moon decided to hide behind heavy clouds, and the darkness is so thick, it envelops me completely. My labored breathing is loud in my ears. I can't see two steps ahead of me, but I shouldn't complain. If I can't see shit, then he can't see me either.

I hear the faint burble of water running over rocks, and I dare to let hope flare in my chest. I'm going in the right direction. The small stream runs parallel to the road. I just have to cross it, and then I'll be a step closer to freedom. I'm so near now that I not only hear the stream but smell the moss that covers the stones near the bank.

Suddenly, the ground disappears from beneath my feet, and I tumble down the hill and land halfway into the stream with a loud splash. I curse my clumsiness as I try to keep the panic from rising. My pulse skyrockets, and I can't perceive any sound besides the pounding in my ears until I hear his mocking voice calling me.

"Isabelle, Isabelle. You can run, but you can't hide from me, *cariño.*"

A whimper escapes my lips, and I hate myself for being weak. His sweet tone puts more fear in my heart than if he had screamed at me in anger or called me names. I remain frozen in place for what feels like an eternity before adrenaline kicks in and I force myself to get up and keep running for my life.

1

NICOLA / ISABELLE

ONE YEAR LATER

J hug the welcome folder tight against my body as I stare at my new school building. My heart shrivels inside my chest. Maverick Prep. Another private school filled with assholes who think they can destroy your life without repercussions. I'd have gone to a big public school where I could disappear in the crowd if the choice had been mine. But my parents felt I'd be safer here.

I touch the long scar across my forehead, now hidden by thick bangs. I almost didn't survive my last school. I was a naive freshman who let the glamour of the wealthy seduce me until it tried to kill me. That girl is gone. Three years have passed since I first met the monster who gave me the scar, but it feels like eons ago.

Things need to be different this time. My parents had to pull a lot of strings to send me to this fancy school in the oceanside town of Triton Cove. The asshole who gave me the scar is still free, probably terrorizing other innocent girls. The fear that he's not done with me is real, hence I had to move across the Atlantic Ocean and change names.

I also had to die.

With a shaky breath, I take a step forward, and another. I can almost hear the ominous soundtrack in the background. Once I enter the automatic doors, I freeze. Panic constricts my airways. Maverick Prep is a replica of my old school. It's not just the modern vibe, or the wide windows in the hallway that let me see inside the classrooms. It's the people. The uniform looks too much like my old one. Same colors—navy with red accents. It didn't dawn on me until now.

I'm going to be sick.

"What the hell are you doing? Move!"

I'm shoved aside by a burly guy with a shaved head. Jesus fucking Christ. So it begins.

An angry retort bubbles up my throat, but I swallow it down. I have to fly under the radar of the popular students here. In my experience, the higher they stand in the school hierarchy, the worse human beings they are.

Someone chuckles. A guy.

I turn with a frown, ready to ask what he finds so funny. Shit, reining in my nature will be hard. He's leaning against the wall with one foot propped against it. He's the definition of tall, dark, and handsome. A little on the pale side for a person living in coastal California, but it suits him. His aquamarine-blue eyes are framed by ridiculously long lashes, but it's his full lips, curled into a grin, that make my heart flutter.

His tie hangs loose around his neck, and his shirt could use some ironing. That carelessly put-together look paired with his messy hair and cocky smile raises alarms in my head. There's no doubt in my mind that he's the top dog here, and I just caught his attention.

6

Crap.

His eyes widen as if he's surprised about something, but then his gaze sharpens, turning dark.

"Fresh meat and already creating trouble." He pushes off the wall and walks over.

"I'm not."

He tilts his head. "You're not fresh meat, or you're not creating trouble?"

I let out a sigh. I can't let him rope me into mind games. "I'd love to stay and chat, but I'm late to see the headmaster," I lie.

"I'll walk with you."

"Why?" The question escapes my lips before I can stop it. Damn it.

He gives me a lopsided grin, showing a hint of teeth. He's like a wolf who's toying with his prey before he pounces. My pulse accelerates, but I'm not sure if it's from fear, excitement, or both.

Isabelle, if you fall for another asshole, then you're seriously messed up in the head.

He smirks. "I don't need a reason."

Of course, he doesn't. He has the attitude of the king of school.

"Jason, babe. I've been looking all over for you." A tall brunette sashays toward us, flanked by two friends in a perfectly executed Beyoncé squad formation.

"We just saw each other," he replies in a bored tone.

I step aside, knowing this chick will become territorial in the blink of an eye.

Her fake smile falters, and then she cuts her cold stare in my direction. I pretend I don't notice her and keep walking. It's a struggle to maintain a normal pace and not sprint down the hallway.

"Who was that weirdo?" she asks loud enough for me to hear.

7

"Don't know. Some new girl."

"What's with her hair? She looks like a Black Veil Brides reject," another girl pipes up.

"Is that a bad thing?" Jason asks with a hint of annoyance.

I turn a corner, and the cacophony of several people speaking at once makes it impossible to keep eavesdropping on their conversation. Not that I care to know what they think about how I look. My jet-black hair and brown contact lenses were some of the changes I had to make, besides using a fake name.

I find my locker and then go straight to my first-period class. Unfortunately, it's advanced Spanish, and I couldn't get out of it. The monster who tried to kill me was from Spain, and every time I hear the language, it makes my skin crawl.

There's an empty chair in the back corner, and that's where I park my butt. Hopefully, no one will notice me. I pull out my cell phone to appear busy and avoid making eye contact with anyone.

I'm not allowed to keep in touch with my old friends or follow them on social media, because it's too risky. But no one can stop me from keeping up with the classical music scene. Before Juan came into my life, I was on the path to becoming one of the greatest violinists in the world—according to my tutors, that is. Now, thanks to needing to keep a low profile, I had to give up my dream. Of all the sacrifices I had to make, that was the hardest.

Glutton for punishment that I am, I decide to watch Seo-Jun Kim's latest performance. She was my biggest competition, and since I was forced to abandon my career, there's no one stopping her from claiming the throne of violin prodigy.

Tears of frustration gather in my eyes, and I'm lost in my pain.

"I didn't peg you for a classical music fan," a voice says near my ear, and even through the AirPods, I can hear Jason clearly. He sounds more annoyed than curious.

I jump in my seat and turn to glare. Big mistake. He's much too close, and I almost bump my nose with his. Quickly, I lean back.

"Have you ever heard of privacy?" I ask.

He smiles, but it's grim, and something inside me shivers a little. "No. And a word of advice—if you have any secrets you'd like to keep, I'd suggest you play nice with me."

The teacher enters the classroom then, prompting Jason to step away and return to his seat far away from me. Thank God he's not my neighbor. Unfortunately, his statement rattled me. I'm still reeling from it when the teacher calls my name.

"Yes?" I blurt out.

"No 'yes,' Señorita Devlin. Nosotros solo hablamos español en clase."

"Perdón."

Everyone is now staring at me, which makes my face heat up like a hot-air balloon. *Hell.*

He asks me to introduce myself to the rest of the class, because I'm starting school a week late. I'm fluent in Spanish, but when I open my mouth to say the rehearsed background story, no words come out. To my dismay, my body begins to shake. Black dots appear in my vision, and then nothing.

2

NICOLA / ISABELLE

*W*hen I wake up, I'm lying on my back, and there's a bright light on the ceiling that hurts my eyes. I try to get up, but a hand on my arm stops me.

"Don't move just yet," Jason says. "Nurse Veronica, your patient is awake."

I turn my head and find him sitting on a chair next to the exam table. Oh no. I must have fainted during Spanish class.

"Did you bring me here?" I ask.

He smiles in an enigmatic way but doesn't answer. It doesn't bring me comfort. It's chilling. A moment later, the nurse opens the partition and walks in.

"How are you feeling, Ms. Devlin?"

"I'm fine."

She watches me through a hard stare. "People who are fine don't faint. Does this happen often?"

Why is she asking me personal questions in front of Jason? Doesn't anyone in this school know the meaning of privacy?

"You have my medical records, so you know the answer to that already," I snap.

Her lips become a thin, flat line. "I see. When was the last time you ate?"

Oh God. Seriously?

I sit up to show her that I really *am* okay. The reason I fainted was psychological, but hell if I'm going to tell her that in front of Jason. Now that I know she couldn't care less about protecting my privacy, she'll get nothing from me, even if the pest is not present.

"I had a good breakfast. Listen, I'm fine. Can I go now?" I jump off the bench.

Dizziness doesn't hit me, probably because no one is forcing me to speak Spanish.

Jason stands and tells the nurse, "I'll escort Nicola to her next class, just in case she's not feeling as great as she claims."

The nurse gives him a nod. "You do that, Jason."

I don't wait for him before I walk out of the nurse's office. I'm glad that once we hit the hallway, there's not a soul in sight. I glance at the clock mounted on the wall; classes are still in progress.

"We have a few minutes before the next period. Let's get some fresh air," Jason says.

If I were smarter, I'd make an excuse not to follow him, but I'm curious about his game. It seems I'm playing it whether I want to or not, so I might as well understand the rules.

"You didn't answer my question. Did you carry me out of Spanish class?"

"Someone had to. I can't believe your nose didn't break. Your face hit the desk pretty hard."

Way to go unnoticed, Isabelle.

I touch my nose, finding it tender. It would have sucked breaking it again. "Small blessings, I guess."

Once outside, Jason leads me to a picnic table that's partially shaded by an oak tree. He sits on the shaded side. No wonder he's pale. Does he ever get any sun?

I slide onto the bench across from him and then endure his scrutinizing stare without flinching.

After a long stretch of silence, he shakes his head and sticks his hand in his jacket pocket.

"Here. Have this." He slides a fruit bar across the table.

I stare at the snack for a couple of beats without moving, taken aback by the offering. With a frown, I lift my face to his. "I said earlier I had a good breakfast."

"So? That means nothing."

I return the snack to him, but before I can pull my hand back, he traps it underneath his, angling his body forward.

"What's your deal, Nicola Devlin?"

Hating how his touch sends a ripple of pleasure up my arm, I yank my hand free. "I could ask you the same thing, Jason."

He narrows his eyes. "You remind me of someone."

I feel the blood drain from my face. He can't possibly know who I am. I look nothing like I used to. Besides the different hair and eye color, my nose was broken, and the doctors couldn't fix it back to how it was. It's different, though not terrible.

"My appearance is pretty ordinary," I say.

"If you say so. Why did you come to Triton Cove?"

"Oh, we're playing the third-degree game now?"

He leans back, smiling like the cat who ate the canary. "You don't like to talk about yourself, do you?"

"No. I'm a private person."

"Or you have something to hide. No one comes to Triton Cove, much less enrolls at Maverick Prep in the middle of the semester, if there isn't some juicy motive behind it."

Damn it. This dude is like a dog with a bone.

"I missed one week of class. That hardly qualifies as middle of the semester," I retort.

"What do your parents do?"

"They're business executives. They live in Europe." The lie rolls off my tongue easily since I rehearsed it so many times.

His eyebrows arch. "Oh, so you're boarding."

I don't like how that information perks him up.

"Yes."

His smile broadens. "Me too."

Great. That means he can harass me during *and* after school.

The bell rings, ending this torturous conversation.

I get up first. "Well, Jason. It's been real, and it's been fun, but I can't say it's been real fun."

3

NICOLA / ISABELLE

*W*hen the first school day is finally over, I'm destroyed mentally and physically. The stress of navigating a new place and avoiding giving too much information about myself was exhausting. I could have done without Jason's attention.

My fainting episode didn't go unnoticed. I bet that Jason taking me to the nurse's office also helped get the rumor mill going. I heard all types of theories, from anorexia to being knocked up. Since those stories are nowhere close to the truth, I don't mind them. I'm sure by the end of the week it will be forgotten.

I must keep my distance from Jason, though. The last thing I need is to be pulled into his orbit.

Once I enter my dorm room, I let out a breath of relief. I can finally relax. I'm one of the lucky few who doesn't have a roommate, and that's thanks to my parents' friendship with the headmaster, whom they've known since they were in high school. He's the only person in Triton Cove who knows Isabelle Maldonaro is still alive.

After the nurse's behavior and Jason's claim that he could uncover all my secrets, I'm not that happy that the headmaster knows my true identity. I'll just have to keep my fingers crossed that Jason never gets hold of that information.

I take off my clothes as I walk to the en suite bathroom, another perk I bet not many students have. The first thing I do is remove my contact lenses. My eyes are dry and burning like a mother. This is the worst part of my disguise. I wish I hadn't worn them today. Now I'm stuck.

My parents insisted it was necessary because my natural eye color is too unique. Not many people in the world have violet eyes like Elizabeth Taylor. I didn't know the lenses would be so uncomfortable.

Next step is to remove the heavy makeup. I never wore much before, but now I need to hide my freckles. When I'm done peeling off all the layers of my disguise, it's like a weight has been removed from my shoulders. I'm finally myself. Okay, my hair is not naturally this dark, but at least it suits me. And I've had time to get used to my new nose.

Knowing that I have a ton of catching up to do, thanks to the week of classes I missed, I hop into the shower so I can snuggle up in bed and do my homework after.

My plan goes up in flames and I almost have a heart attack when I walk out of the bathroom and find Jason chilling on my bed with his hands linked behind his head.

I let out a scream and almost lose the towel wrapped around my body. Panic sets in and I begin to hyperventilate.

"Jesus, what's wrong with you?" He jumps out of bed and walks over.

Clutching my towel, I glare at the asshole. "What's… wrong… with *me?*"

He places his hands on my arms as if he wants to help me stay upright. "Just breathe."

I'd push him off if I wasn't busy trying to draw air into my lungs. I'm wheezing, and it's embarrassing as hell. Although, I shouldn't feel this way when he's the one responsible for my panic attack.

His thumbs make small circles over my skin. It's a soothing motion that does things to my body. I hold his stare, grateful that his eyes are nothing like Juan's. It doesn't look like Jason is breathing as he watches me. But his eyes seem to burn with fury for a moment, contradicting what his hands are doing to me.

It takes me a minute to recover the ability to breathe properly. When I do, I step away from him.

"You… how…"

The emotion shining in his gaze vanishes, and he shrugs. "I knocked. You didn't answer it, so I used my master key."

"You have a *master key?*" I shriek.

"Are you going to repeat everything I say?"

I'm feeling dizzy, so I make a beeline to my bed and sit down. "What the hell is wrong with you? You can't simply barge into somebody's room."

"I was worried. You *did* faint earlier." He gives me an innocent smile.

Worried my ass.

"Well, congratulations. You almost made me faint again."

"Was that why you passed out earlier? Because you were having a panic attack?"

Shit. I've said too much.

"What do you want?" I grit out.

"I already told you. I came to check on you." He cocks his head. "Are you wearing colored contact lenses?"

Ah crap. I forgot I removed my lenses before the shower. But he thinks my natural color is brown... "Yes."

"It suits you. And you shouldn't wear so much makeup to hide your freckles. Guys prefer the more natural look."

My eyebrows arch. "Aren't you conceited and a half? You think whatever women do is to please men, don't you?"

He chuckles. "Am I wrong?"

"Yes," I hiss. "I couldn't care less what you think."

"So, are you saying you hate yourself so much that you need to cover your face with layers of chemicals?"

This dude is seriously pissing me off. To hell with playing nice. I jump from the bed and stride toward him, stopping only when I'm in his space.

"I don't hate myself. I hate arrogant asses who think the world revolves around them."

The amused grin vanishes from his lips. His eyes narrow, turning intense as he stares into mine. I make a motion to step back, but he grabs my chin, forcing me to maintain eye contact as he studies me. The rough grip triggers bad memories, but at the same time, his touch is electrifying in a good way.

What am I thinking? Did my horrific experience fuck me up in the head?

"Those are amazing contacts, Nicola. They look real." He releases me and steps back. "Have you ever played an instrument, by any chance?"

His change of subject makes my head spin. "What?"

"The violin, perhaps?" He quirks an eyebrow.

My stomach turns into knots as my pulse skyrockets. *Oh my God, he recognizes me.*

"No. What prompted that question?"

He shrugs. "You were watching one of the best young violinists in the world. It was a safe guess."

I exhale and pray he doesn't notice my relief. "Well, you guessed wrong." I cross my arms.

17

"All right, then. I'd better go. Don't want you to get in trouble for having a male guest in your room."

His eyes flash with a devilish glint before he walks out, leaving the door ajar.

Fucking asshole.

4

NICOLA / ISABELLE

*D*espite my attempt to keep to myself and not befriend anyone, when a shy, dark-haired girl as pale as the moon breaks the ice by complimenting my shoes, I don't have the heart to brush her off.

"Thanks," I say, fixing my bangs to make sure they're in place. "I'm Isa—Nicola. What's your name?"

"Sage Halle," she replies with a small smile.

Hmm, I guess people like to say their last names here. That wasn't the case in Europe. "Nice to meet you."

"Are you new?"

"Yes, it's my second day."

"Where did you transfer from?"

I become tongue tied. I can't tell her I spent a year in and out of hospitals and was taught by private tutors for my entire junior year. I also can't tell her I went to school in Barcelona before that.

"Eh…"

Her attention switches from me to a good-looking guy who just walked into the cafeteria. He's tall and athletic, with tanned skin, dark curls, and bright-green eyes that have all the girls in the vicinity turning their heads.

He ignores them all and makes a beeline toward us. "Hey, Sage. What's up?"

"Not much," she replies softly.

Her cheeks are bright red, and I feel sorry for her. It sucks when your body betrays you like that.

He looks at me. "Hi, I'm Justice."

No last name. Interesting.

"Nicola."

The line moves, and that gives me an excuse to not engage in conversation with him. It seems Justice is more interested in chatting with Sage anyway, so I get a reprieve.

It doesn't last long, and this time, it's not Jason pestering me.

"Didn't I already tell you to stay away from my sister?" an angry male voice asks.

I turn and see a blond guy glowering at Justice. He's shorter than him, and my guess is a couple of years younger, but he doesn't seem one bit fazed by that.

"I was just saying hello. Is that a crime now?" Justice replies almost mockingly.

"Luke, cut it out." Sage tries to push her brother away from Justice, but he's like a boulder, unmovable.

I take note of two other guys hovering nearby. They look to be about the same age as Sage's brother, either freshmen or sophomores. One of them has chin-length, wavy, blond hair and the body of a swimmer. I notice him first because he looks kind of familiar.

"What's going on here?" Jason asks, appearing out of nowhere.

He glowers at Justice and Luke, then turns to the guy with long hair. "Get your friends in line, Finn."

Finn arches his eyebrows. "Do you think I can control Luke?"

Jason rolls his eyes and sighs. "Children."

He grabs Justice by the back of his collar and drags him away from the line. "All right, perv. Time for you to stop sniffing around the kindergarten."

"Let go of me!" Justice tries to break free, but his effort is half hearted. I suspect he's trying to save face but knows it'd be a mistake to truly antagonize Jason.

"You suck, Luke," Sage snaps.

His gaze softens. "I'm just looking out for you. He's too old."

"He's only a couple years older than me. But it's not really his age that's bothering you, is it? You don't like him because he's poor."

Luke's eyes widen. He looks truly shocked. "I don't like him because he's shady."

Sage pushes him out of her way and strides out of the cafeteria. I debate whether I should follow her, but the decision is made for me when Jason returns to the line. I want to know what he did to Justice.

"Did you kick his ass?" the dark-haired guy in the group asks.

"No, Cameron. I didn't kick his ass. My methods are more subtle than brute force. Take note."

"Whatever," he mumbles.

The trio makes a motion to leave, but Jason steps next to Finn and gives him a side hug.

"Congrats, cuz."

A-ha. That's why he looked familiar. Now that Jason is standing next to him, I can see the resemblance.

"Thanks. I didn't know you went to the meet."

"Of course, I did. I knew Uncle Dearest wouldn't be there, and your mom... well, you never know with her."

Finn turns his blue eyes in my direction, and a blush creeps up his cheeks. It seems Jason doesn't know how to keep *anyone's* secrets, not even his family's.

Finn looks away. "Right. I'd better go."

Hoping that Jason is still distracted by his cousin, I slink away from him, following the flow of the line. I grab a tray and slide it along the counter as I check the food offerings. Wishful thinking that I'd be able to escape him so easily.

He falls into step with me. "Did you enjoy the show?"

"No, but it got my attention."

He leans closer, brushing his arm with mine. "What didn't you like about it?" His voice is low and seductive, as if he's trying to tease me.

Goose bumps spread where he touched me, despite the barrier of clothes. My body is reacting to his proximity in ways I can't control, and I hate it.

"Your attitude, maybe?"

He laughs. "Oh, so you support grooming then?"

I frown. "Justice was just chatting with Sage."

"Right, like I just want to chat with you."

My heart skips a beat and I falter in my step. "Is that what you're hoping to achieve?"

He tilts his head, smiling that crooked smile of his while his eyes dance with mischief. "You have to be more specific, darling."

I clench my jaw hard. "You'd better forget it. I'm not going to fuck you."

His smile doesn't wilt. In fact, I think he's trying hard to not let it become broader. "We'll see. But anyway, I didn't come to the cafeteria to run interference in my cousin and his friends' business."

"Do I dare ask why you're here, then?" I put random food on my tray, knowing I won't feel like eating anything.

"It's a surprise." He takes the tray from me and sets it back on the counter. "Come."

Grabbing my hand, he drags me away from the line. "What the hell. What about my food?"

"You're weird, but no one in their right mind eats tofu gumbo."

Good grief. Was that what I picked?

Why are you surprised, Isabelle, when his nearness is giving you all sorts of crazy reactions?

I try to ignore how his possessive hand clasping mine is making me warm and cold at the same time. I know he's trouble, but I want to ignore the signs.

People are staring at me again. Most are curious, except the girl who spoke to Jason when I first arrived, who looks like she's about to murder me.

"Where are we going?" I ask.

"I want to show you something."

I let him steer me down the hallway, and not once do I try to pull free from his grasp. I'm enjoying the connection too much, which is proof that I'm insane. Jason has all the markings of a psycho. Why am I not repelled by his proximity?

We enter a large empty room, and I have to suppress a gasp. It's the music classroom. I'm flooded by emotions, both happy and bitter. I forget that Jason is there for a moment as I let go of his hand to walk farther in. My chest feels heavy, and I massage it with my fist, trying to ease the ache.

I turn to ask Jason why he brought me here, but he's gone.

What in the world? I don't understand the game he's playing, but I don't care to analyze his motives right now. I see a violin case on a desk and head straight for it. Against my parents' wishes, I packed my violin only to discover that it never made it to California. They must have found it in my belongings and taken it out. I understand why they did it. I wouldn't have been able not to play it otherwise. It doesn't mean their decision didn't leave a gaping hole in my chest.

I run my fingers over the smooth wooden case, and with shaking hands, I lift the lid. It's a Benedicte Friedmann Stradivari violin. Like a junkie unable to contain herself, I remove the instrument and rest it on my shoulder. Before I know it, I'm in the middle of Vivaldi's *Four Seasons*, which is the composition that got me into classical music.

My heart soars as I become lost in the sound. I feel alive again. I close my eyes for a moment, but when I pivot, they're open, and I find Jason standing there, watching me with so much hatred in his eyes that it sucks the joy out of me.

A woman enters the room as I'm lowering the bow.

"Oh my God," she says.

Jason turns to her, and the glower turns into surprise. The woman doesn't acknowledge him.

"I'm sorry. I didn't mean to… I'll put it back."

"Oh, no. You can't put it back. You must keep playing."

Panic rises up my throat. I can't play. If I do, he'll find me.

I shake my head. "I… I can't."

"Nonsense. I've never had a student with such talent before."

"Excuse me?" Jason butts in.

She glances at him. "Oh, I'm sorry, Jason. You're very talented, of course, but her… she's divine!"

The full-on hate returns to his eyes. His nostrils flare, and his jaw is locked so tightly, I'm afraid he'll shatter his teeth. It looks like he's about to explode.

"You must join my class. I insist," the woman continues.

The *no* is on the tip of my tongue, even though saying it will likely kill me a bit more. I shouldn't have played the violin. I couldn't play while in the hospital, and when I finally went home, I was too depressed to practice. Then I traveled to Triton Cove and discovered my violin was missing. But now that I've tasted the euphoria again, I can't give it up. I don't want to give it up. Practicing at school shouldn't be a big deal. It's participating in competitions that would put me in danger. Maybe that makes me too stupid to live, but what I have now isn't much of a life. I need something to motivate me to keep going, to prevent my own darkness from consuming me whole.

"She can't join," Jason grits out.

I had already almost convinced myself that forgetting the violin forever was a fate too cruel to bear. But seeing how much he's bothered by me joining the class is the push I need to do something reckless but ultimately right for me.

I watch him through narrowed eyes for a few seconds before I turn to the teacher. "It'll be an honor to join your class."

5

NICOLA / ISABELLE

*J*ason leaves me alone the next day, and his absence is beginning to give me anxiety. He's plotting something. That look of pure hatred he gave me was not normal. It should have terrified me, considering my past. But it somehow gave me strength. I'm not cowering in front of another asshole god.

It's not until my first class with Mrs. Simpson, the music teacher, that I see him again. I had to give up a free period to join. He's in this class. Sadly, so is his friend from the hallway on my first day, whose name, I've learned, is Sloane. Great.

"Good morning, everyone. I'd like you to meet Nicola Devlin. She'll be joining our program."

"Why? I thought we were full," Sloane retorts.

"There's always room for remarkable talent. Trust me, we all gain by the addition of Ms. Devlin."

Hell, way to make everyone here hate me, Mrs. Simpson.

"What instrument does she play?" a freckled guy with thick glasses asks.

"The violin," I answer, sick of people talking about me as if I weren't in the room.

The guy grimaces, then turns to Jason.

"We already have a badass violinist." Sloane crosses her arms.

"No one else plays the violin here?" I ask.

A couple of people raise their hands timidly.

"They don't count." Sloane turns and gives them the death glare.

Everything becomes crystal clear to me then. Jason is the first chair violin. Maybe if I hadn't been busy having an inner argument, it would have dawned on me sooner. No wonder he almost lost his mind when Mrs. Simpson gushed over me and didn't want me to join her class. He's been getting all the solos. If I'm better, that will go away.

I don't get it. Why did he bring me to this room in the first place? What was he hoping to gain?

"If Nicola is so good, let's hear it, then," Sloane replies with a smirk.

She's challenging me, and that sends a rush of excitement through my veins. As crazy as it sounds, I've missed the competitiveness of performing arts. *No, you can't go there, Isabelle. You're just going to practice.* There's only one issue.

"I don't have a violin," I say with regret.

Sloane snorts. "What kind of violinist doesn't have their own instrument?"

"It got stolen on the trip here," I lie.

Not that I owe her an explanation, but it *is* strange that I don't have a violin. I don't want anyone thinking too much about it. It's bad enough that Jason asked me point blank if I played, and I lied to him. He said he was going to unveil all my secrets, and now he knows I have a closetful of them.

"She can use mine. I mean, she already helped herself to it the other day," Jason chimes in.

That was *his* violin? Why did he leave such an expensive instrument in the classroom? More and more, I'm beginning to suspect Jason set a trap for me, but the outcome was not what he expected. It doesn't matter. The nagging suspicion that he knows who I am makes me sick to my stomach. If he's angry that I might take his place as the star of the show, there's nothing stopping him from unveiling my secret. But I know if I stop playing altogether, I'll return to the bleakness I experienced during my recovery. That's almost as scary as the prospect of Juan finding me. I'm stuck between a rock and a hard place.

"I didn't know it was yours," I grit out.

He smiles but it has no warmth. "Now you do."

I watch him take the instrument from its case and then walk across the room to hand it over. He leans closer and whispers in my ear. "Enjoy the spotlight while you can, Nicola. It won't last."

I hate that his threat makes my body tremble a little. It's not that I'm afraid of him. I fear the devil he might send after me.

"Do you have a specific request?" I ask Mrs. Simpson.

"Surprise me," she replies with a smile.

I don't want to show off, and it's been a while since I've practiced. I decide to play a piece I'm familiar with. Beethoven's Violin Sonata No. 5. It's strange now to be playing the instrument, knowing it belongs to Jason. It feels intimate.

I get into position and then make the mistake of looking at him. His aquamarine-blue eyes are as dark as a thunderstorm. It sends a shiver down my spine. I don't know what I did to earn that rage from him. Getting angry because he has to share the spotlight feels excessive, even for a spoiled asshole.

Trying to ground myself, I look away first and begin. The notes aren't as sharp as I know I can play them, but I'm not terrible. Unfortunately, I can't lose myself in the music completely today. An audience never unsettled me before, but Jason alone is doing that to me.

When I finish, Mrs. Simpson claps enthusiastically. Everyone else remains frozen, half the room staring at me and the other half at Jason. His expression is closed off. He could be mistaken for a marble statue.

My heart is hammering madly inside my chest as I walk over to return his violin. He holds my stare as he takes the instrument from me.

"Thank you," I say.

He doesn't reply. *Fine. You want to be rude? Be my guest.*

I find a seat across the room and far away from him. My head is filled with theories and questions about his behavior, so I barely hear what Mrs. Simpson is saying. Each student plays a short solo, and then the class is over.

Jason is the first out of the room. Sloane scrambles to follow him and ends up dropping half the contents of her bag on the floor. No one offers to help her pick them up.

On my way out, Mrs. Simpson stops me. "You need a new violin as soon as possible, Ms. Devlin. We have a recital in a month, and I'd love for you to play a duet with Jason."

"Uh, what?" My voice comes out as a squeak.

"Are you deaf?" Sloane asks on her way to the door.

She doesn't wait for my reply—not that I'd be able to offer a retort in my current freaking-out state of mind. I wasn't expecting to perform so soon. It wouldn't be a big deal. This is a small town, and I doubt the press would be interested in covering the event. I think it's the idea of a duet with Jason that's making me nervous.

"We have a recital to celebrate the beginning of the school year. It's also a charity event. Usually, Jason has a solo, but I think it would be a breath of fresh air if we have a duet this time. You'd be amazing together."

"Uh, I don't know. It's such short notice. Maybe we should let him have the solo this time."

She tilts her head. "Are you intimidated by him because of who his mother is?"

"Should I know who she is?"

"Oh dear. She's Victoria Petrov."

My eyes bug out. "The pianist?"

Mrs. Simpson nods. "The one and only. As you might know, she retired from playing professionally when she married into the Novak family. She's still a legend though."

"I had no idea. Is Jason's family a big deal, I mean, the Novaks?"

"Oh, I forget you're brand new to Triton Cove. Yes, they are a big deal. They founded the town—one might say they own it."

No wonder Jason acts the way he does.

"Well, good. Then it's all settled." Mrs. Simpson continues.

"Have you asked Jason if he's okay with it?"

She furrows her eyebrows. "I understand that Jason is some type of king among the students, but he has no say in my classroom."

She can't force me to perform, and I know Jason is going to make my life miserable. But practicing with him will maybe shed light on his behavior. Keep your enemies close and all that.

NICOLA / ISABELLE

I hoped I wouldn't see Jason for the rest of the day, but during study hall, he finds me in the library.

He pulls up a chair next to mine and leans his right elbow on the table, angling his body so he's facing me. "I just received the news I'm to partner with you for a duet."

He seems less edgy, but his eyes are bloodshot, and the scent of *eau de cannabis* emanates from him. No wonder he's not giving me a death glare.

"I tried to get out of it."

Why did I tell him that?

"Because you think you're too good to play a duet?"

"No, because I don't want to play at a recital. I haven't practiced in months," I grit out.

He sits straighter. "You're a filthy little liar, aren't you, Nicola?"

My face becomes hot in a flash. "I'm not lying."

"Oh, I think you are. You lied to me about never having played the violin before. Is anything that comes out of your mouth real?"

I can't answer that truthfully. I look away. "I'm busy. If you only came here to—"

He slaps his hand on the table hard, making me jerk in my seat. "Do not dismiss me, Nicola. I can make your life very unpleasant here at Maverick Prep."

His eyes shine with a dangerous glint. I was fooled into believing pot could tame the beast.

"What do you want from me? Can't you just leave me alone?"

He stands up. "You should have said no to Mrs. Simpson. Now we have to spend every spare moment together, practicing for the recital, and I'll make sure to take some pleasure from it one way or another."

I WANT to call my parents so badly, but our calls must be scheduled, and they need to use burner phones to make sure the calls aren't traceable. Juan's family is that powerful. If Jason's family owns Triton Cove, Juan's family owns Europe. My attack was never mentioned anywhere, and my cause of death was a hit-and-run. Pushing for justice would mean destroying my parents' lives. They would lose their jobs, their reputation. Juan's father would make sure they were nothing but dust. It would all be for nothing, because no judge in Spain would convict Juan. I couldn't do that to them. In the end, it was my decision to fake my death and start over. It doesn't mean it's not hard. I can never go back to being Isabelle Maldonaro.

My parents want me to be safe, and they resigned themselves that their only daughter has died for real. But playing the violin made me feel alive again, and I can't bear to give up that feeling. I'll stand up to Jason, and any other bully who gets in my way. I survived worse than him—much, much worse.

Before I take a shower, I prop my chair against the door, something I've been doing since Jason made himself at home in my room. Unfortunately, I can't keep him from breaking in when I'm not around. I hid anything that could clue him in about my true identity, but I'm still paranoid he's going to find something I missed.

I'm barely out of the shower when a loud knock on my door disturbs my peace.

What now?

I look through the peephole, and sure as shit, there's Jason. I bet he tried to barge in like before.

"What do you want?" I ask through the closed door.

"I have a gift for you," he replies sweetly.

"Leave it outside then."

"What's the matter, Nicola? Are you afraid of me?"

Stupid, cocky asshole. He knows exactly how to manipulate me. I yank the door open, forgetting to put clothes on first. Once again, I'm standing in front of him wearing nothing but a towel.

He raises an eyebrow. "Are you already trying to get on my good side, Nicola?"

"Don't flatter yourself. You have terrible timing."

He walks in, carrying a violin case in his hand. It has a big red bow on top.

"What's that?"

"Your gift." He sets the case on the bed.

Crossing my arms, I glower. "Unnecessary. I can buy my own instrument."

"Sure. But you're going to use this one. Go on. Open it."

There's a challenge in his eyes. He won't leave my room until I do as he says, and sadly, I can't force him out. In a brute force contest, he wins.

I yank the bow from the top and then unlatch the box. Inside a bright-pink velvet interior lies the most outrageous, rainbow-colored violin.

"What the hell is this?"

"You don't like it? I figured to balance out your drab coloring, a bit of color would be nice."

"I can't use this. It's ridiculous."

His gaze sharpens. "You can and you will. Now get dressed. We're late for practice."

I shut the violin case and then shove it against his chest. "I'm not using this."

He grabs my arms, pulling me closer. The hard case presses against my breasts. "You're under the impression you have a choice."

"I *do* have a choice. I won't allow you to bully me. I'm not afraid of you, Jason."

He leans forward, bringing his face inches from mine. "You should be afraid of me, *Isabelle*."

7

NICOLA / ISABELLE

The ground seems to vanish beneath my feet while the room begins to spin. If Jason hadn't been holding me, I think I'd have collapsed.

"What did you call me?" I ask through the lump in my throat.

His lips curl into a cruel grin. "You heard me. Your real name is Isabelle Maldonaro. And you're supposed to be dead."

I shake my head, the denial on the tip of my tongue. But Jason can see the tears that are welling up in my eyes and the glint of desperation that's surely shining in them. I step back, pulling myself free of him.

"I don't know what you're talking about. My name is Nicola Devlin," I reply feebly.

"What I want to know is why the most promising violinist in Europe, and perhaps the world, would fake her own death and move to Triton Cove," he continues, rubbing his chin as if pondering hard.

I curl my hands into fists, digging my nails into my palms until it hurts. "I'm not Isabelle."

He tosses the violin case to the side and strides toward me. I tense to run, but he's upon me before I can, holding my chin firmly like he did the last time he was in my room.

"Stop lying to me," he grits out.

My pulse accelerates to the max, but also adrenaline has kicked in. I shove him off me with all my strength. He staggers back, stunned for a moment.

"I don't owe you anything," I say.

Instead of his face twisting into an expression of rage, a cold and calculating mask falls in place instead. "No, but you're pretending to be someone else for a reason. Don't expect that to remain a secret for much longer." He walks to the door.

My stomach bottoms out a second later. I have no reason to believe he's bluffing.

Shit, Isabelle. You can't let him spill the beans.

"Jason, wait."

He stops, but he doesn't turn. "Yes?"

"You can't say anything."

Slowly, he looks over his shoulder. "Why is that?"

"Because I'm asking you not to."

Laughing, he shakes his head. "I don't know if you're naive or only playing at it. Let me save you the time. I don't have a nice side you can appeal to. If you want me to keep your secret, you'll have to pay for my silence."

"You want money?" My voice rises in pitch.

"Darling, I come from grotesque money." He walks to my bed and flops onto it, getting comfortable. "I want you to play for me."

I stare at him without blinking.

"That's it? You want me to play."

"For now."

I clench my jaw. Of all the things I thought he was going to ask, that wasn't it. Probably because it's too easy.

"I have to get dressed first."

"No. You'll play for me like that."

I knew it. He knows there's a chance I might lose my towel while playing. I know better now than trying to convince him to let me put clothes on. He wants to torture me.

I retrieve the color-explosion violin from its case and start by tuning it. This takes a while, but Jason doesn't seem to be in a hurry. He's watching my every move with a satisfied smirk on his face.

Content that I won't sound like nails scratching a blackboard, I get in position.

"Any requests?"

"Play something by Mendelssohn." He links his hands behind his head.

I start playing *Allegro Molto Appassionato* and immediately wince at the low quality of the sound. It's probably fine for the untrained ear, but to me, who's played on the best instruments in the world, this is pure agony. Only another violinist would know to pick this type of punishment.

I don't understand why Jason was obsessed with finding out my secret, or why he's so angry that I kept my identity hidden. I can't let him keep digging and discover the reason I went to the extreme of faking my own death. I have no idea if his family has any connection to Juan's. Even if the chances are slim, I can't risk it.

I'm almost done with the piece when the towel begins to slide down. I miss a note, and the violin's shriek hurts my ears.

"Don't you dare stop," he warns me.

So that was his end goal all along. He was hoping for a towel mishap, and that's exactly what happens in the next second. It falls in a heap by my feet. I'm mortified, but I keep my eyes closed so at least I can pretend I'm alone. I refuse to cry in front of him, but my eyes prickle behind my eyelids. The cursed lenses don't help matters either.

Finally, the music ends, but before I open my eyes again, the door shuts with a loud bang.

Jason is gone.

8

JASON

J was enjoying my little torture session. I knew that damn towel wouldn't stay in place while Isabelle played. I didn't expect my body to react the way it did when it finally dropped. I'm not a perv who gets a hard-on every time I see a naked girl. But seeing Isabelle in her birthday suit while she played on that cheap violin made me so hard, I had to escape before she could see what it did to me.

I rush into my room and shut the door with a bang. Like Isabelle, I also have a private bathroom. I refuse to pleasure myself, knowing she's the reason for my current state. I yank off my clothes as I head to the shower, not caring if I rip seams or lose buttons. I set the shower to cold and walk right under the icy jets. It makes me tense and I grind my teeth. But my fucking dick is still standing at attention.

What the hell!

I close my eyes and try to think of anything but her. It's

impossible. Automatically, my hand finds my shaft and I begin to work it, bracing my arm against the cold tiled wall. I don't use any soap to make it easier, I want it to chafe. I'm jerking off to the girl I've hated for nearly a decade.

She has no idea who I am. Why would she remember a scrawny, nobody violinist when she was a prodigy? I used to look up to her, that was until my mother pulled some strings and arranged for me to compete in the same contest as her.

I grunt as I near climax. My balls are tight, ready to explode. Because I'm a glutton for punishment, the last image of Isabelle playing the violin comes to the forefront of my mind, and then my fantasy takes over. I don't run away; instead, I push her against the wall and fuck her until she forgets both her names.

The orgasm hits me then, and it's intense. I don't remember a hand job ever doing this to me, even when performed by someone else. My breathing is still coming out in bursts minutes after I've finished.

I turn off the shower. There's no point in freezing my ass when it didn't do jack to help me out.

I'm drying my hair with a towel when my phone rings. It's *Mozart's Symphony No. 5*, which means my mother is calling. It's easy to guess what she wants to talk about. I can't deal with that bullshit right now. Thank fuck she hates Triton Cove and comes to town only when a family event demands it.

I let it go to voice mail and get dressed. Five minutes later, she calls again. For fuck's sake. Better get this over with.

"What?" I snap. I'm too pissed to play nice.

"Do not 'what' me, Jason. I'm your mother. Show some respect."

I pinch the bridge of my nose and count to ten in my head. "I'm busy. What do you want?"

"I'm in town and unfortunately was roped into dinner with your uncle and grandfather."

"So?" I ask only to be a pest.

I know exactly what she wants now. She can't stand my uncle or grandpa, and the feeling is mutual on their part.

"Dinner is at seven. Be punctual."

She ends the call, not giving me the chance to come up with an excuse not to go. Those dinners are boring as hell. Grandpa is fine, but I detest my uncle. He's an asshole who treats his wife and children like they're props to make him look better.

Sadly, this whole town is made of people like him. My father wasn't much different, but at least he had the balls to marry someone outside of our family's network. If only he had chosen better and not married a viper.

I DRIVE up to my uncle's mansion early but stay in the car because my mother is already there. It's rare that she's punctual, which means she's most likely taking advantage of my uncle's bar. She isn't as bad as Finn's mother. Auntie Marissa is a raging alcoholic. My family life is fucked up, but my cousin has it worse than I do. At least I don't live at home.

The rumble of Finn's sports car brings me back to the here and now. He parks right in front of the house. I might as well walk in with him. He's still wearing sweatpants and a Maverick Sharks T-shirt, and his hair is wet. He probably just came home from swim practice.

He hoists his duffel bag over his shoulder and waits for me to walk over.

"What's up, cuz?" I hug him sideways.

"Not much. What time is this thing?"

I chuckle. "You're the one who lives here, and you don't know?"

The corners of his lips twist upward. "I was in the pool the whole afternoon. I know nothing."

"You have five minutes to get presentable."

He rolls his eyes. "God. That's your mother's car, isn't it?"

"Yep." I throw my arm over his shoulder. "Come on. We can get through this together, then after, we should head to Playground."

His eyes widen. "Dude, I've tried to get into that place since it opened. No amount of dropping names and bribery worked."

"Yeah, they're trying to keep the young crowd away. But I know the owner. I'll get you in."

"Can you also get Luke, Reid, and Cam in? They'd kill me if I went without them."

I sigh, resigned. Finn is tight with those boys. They're the three Musketeers to his D'Artagnan. "If I must. Come on. Let's get this torture over with."

No sooner do I step foot inside, than I hear my mother's annoying voice. Finn quickly disappears up the stairs, leaving me alone to face the monsters.

"Good evening," I say as I enter one of the living rooms.

This is where the cocktails are served before dinner, but as usual, it seems Aunt Marissa has been here for hours. Her eyes are already glazed.

The first thing Mom does is look at her watch. "You're late."

I quirk an eyebrow. "Your watch must be running fast."

Grandpa and Uncle Florian walk into the room, but I get a warm greeting only from Grandpa.

He pulls me into a hug. "Jason, my boy. It's good to see you."

"Hi, Grandpa."

He pulls back but keeps his hands fastened on my arms. "You've grown since the last time I saw you."

"I doubt that."

"So, tell me what's new with you? Did you join any teams this year?"

I open my mouth to reply, but Mom beats me to it. "Jason doesn't have time for sports. God knows he needs to spend all his free time in the music room."

And so it begins.

Uncle Florian snorts. "That's exactly what we need. A Novak in the performing arts. My brother must be twitching in his grave."

"Unlike you, Joseph didn't think less of my profession."

"And yet, didn't you give up playing the piano when you married him?" He brings his glass to his lips, but I can still see his cruel smile.

As much as I like seeing someone stand up to my mother when the subject is me, this is the last place I want to be. "I'm going to check on Finn," I say.

"Not so fast, Jason. I want to talk to you about a disturbing email I received from Mrs. Simpson. Instead of a solo, it seems you're playing a duet with a new student at the recital. How in the world did you let that happen?"

Let that happen. As if I had a choice in the matter.

It's true that my actions put Isabelle on Mrs. Simpson's radar, so in a way, it's my fault she joined the group. When I set the trap for her, I wanted to confirm my suspicions that she was Isabelle Maldonaro. I didn't plan for Mrs. Simpson to barge into the room.

"I don't see the problem," I reply.

My mother's eyes flash. "You've been the solo violinist for the past three years. Now you're going to let a nobody take away the spotlight? Just like you let that insipid girl take away the apprenticeship with Carlos Ferrera all those years ago."

I curl my hands into fists, but it does nothing to keep the rage from taking control. That was my chance to prove to my mother I was as talented as her. She only ever seemed to care about that. But I choked, played like shit, and not only lost that opportunity, but was never considered for anything important again. I became a joke.

"She's not taking away the spotlight. We're sharing it," I grit out.

"Great artists don't share anything." She seethes.

My uncle laughs. "When is it going to dawn on you that your son isn't a prodigy, Victoria?"

Her eyes glare. The walls in this room are caving in, and everything is getting ready to blow. Fuck me. I need to get out of here.

"I think Jason is very talented," Aunt Marissa pipes up.

"I agree," Finn says as he joins the war zone.

"Where the hell have you been?" his father asks.

"I was upstairs changing clothes."

Uncle Florian drains his drink, and not missing a beat, refills the glass almost to the brim.

"I'd like to meet this girl while I'm in town," Mom pipes up. "Bring her to the house tomorrow, Jason."

Hell. The last thing I want is for my mother to meet Isabelle. What if she recognizes her? Knowing her secret is too good of a trump card. I don't want to lose the upper hand, since I just started having fun with her.

"What makes you think we're friends?"

She gives me a droll stare. "I don't expect you to be. But she knows who I am. She won't pass up the opportunity to meet a legend."

Uncle Florian snorts. "Aren't you full of yourself? You're a has-been. No one knows who you are, dear."

Her glare intensifies, and I know they're a second away from starting an ugly argument. But Grandpa steps between them.

"Enough with this bickering. I'm ready to fucking eat." He turns to my aunt. "Stop drowning in vodka and get the staff to serve dinner already, Marissa."

Finn winces but knows better than to say anything in his mother's defense. For starters, he idolizes Grandpa, and like everyone in this room, he's aware of Aunt Marissa's alcohol problem.

I step closer to him and whisper, "I don't know about you, but I've lost my appetite."

For more reasons than one, but mostly because there isn't a way out of introducing Isabelle to my mother, which means giving her the opportunity to find my weaknesses. I can't allow that.

9

NICOLA / ISABELLE

*L*ast night after Jason left my room, I panicked and packed all my stuff. He's not going to share my secret yet, but what happens when he gets tired of playing with me or demands more than I can give?

But seeing my room stripped bare and the little I have left in suitcases made something snap inside of me. I can't let Jason destroy my second chance at having a life. I also can't keep running. I have to stand up to him.

It took me a while to unpack, and by the time I got to bed, I was too exhausted to think about my problems.

On my way to grab breakfast before class, I have an epiphany. The best way to deal with Jason without getting hurt is to discover why he hates me so much. I know there are people who don't need reasons to be cruel. Juan was the perfect example. But I saw Jason interact with his cousin and his cousin's friends. He cares about them. And he brought me to the nurse when I fainted that first day.

A psychopath wouldn't do any of that.

There's a deli near campus that sells the most amazing sandwiches, and the coffee is good. No wonder it's a popular spot among Maverick students. I have time, so I decide to eat outside. Most people are taking food to go.

I'm not wearing my brown contact lenses this morning, so I keep my sunglasses on. The lenses are in my purse so I can put them on in my car before I head to class. My eyes need a serious break from them.

I wish I could say I'm not on edge anymore, but there's a tension in my body that won't go away. I pull my phone out and stick the AirPods in my ears. Maybe some classical music will help me calm down. Nervous people don't make good decisions. I need to bring my *A* game if I'm to win the war against Jason.

It takes me a while, but eventually, the music helps me relax. I'm lost in my bubble, enjoying breakfast, when the bane of my existence pulls up a chair and sits across from me.

I look up and glower. "This is getting old."

He smiles. "Good morning to you too."

"What do you want now?"

"Chill. I'm just here for breakfast."

I notice then that he indeed has a tray of food in front of him. It's greasy and smells delicious—better than mine actually. I went with a healthier option. Jason loaded up on bacon, eggs, and sausage. His cup of coffee is larger than mine too.

Taking into account his food choices and his messier-than-usual look, I can guess he had a wild evening yesterday. "Rough night?"

"You can say that."

He takes a huge bite of his sandwich, and half of it spills out, smearing egg all over his face. I find myself staring at him as if

I'm in a daze. Damn him for looking sexy when he should look like a slob.

"Whuh?" he asks with his mouth half full.

I shake my head and focus on my food. "Nothing."

"Were you thinking about your little performance last night?"

A blush creeps up from my neck to my cheeks. "No, but thanks for reminding me of that. It's exactly the kind of memory I need to start the day on a bright note."

"Confess. You loved playing for me in your birthday suit."

I roll my eyes. "How much more immature can you get?"

He sits straighter and amusement dances in his eyes. Shit, I don't like how perked up he just got. I was trying to make him believe he *didn't* get in my head.

"Are you challenging me, darling?"

"Oh my God. It wasn't a dare!" I add quickly.

"Too late." He smirks, but his smile vanishes quickly, and his gaze darkens. "Why do you want the world to believe you're dead, Isabelle?"

The bite I just took drops heavily into my stomach. I knew he wouldn't let me forget that he knows my secret. Nervous, I look around. There's no one near enough to have overheard him.

"It's better if you don't know," I say.

"You don't get to decide that for me, sweetheart."

I don't know all the rules of his game, but I'm beginning to learn.

"I don't want to tell you. How much is that going to cost me?"

His eyebrows shoot up to the heavens, but after his initial surprise ebbs away, a calculating gleam shines in his eyes. "You're learning. Good for you, Isabelle."

I narrow my gaze. "If you keep calling me that, you'll lose your leverage over me quickly."

He leans back in his chair. "There's something I want from you. It's my price to not ask why I'm talking to a ghost. It'll buy you only one day of reprieve, though."

My hands curl into fists. Of course he's going to milk it. "What do you want?"

"You'll be my plus-one at dinner with my mother tonight."

I was expecting something horrible and depraved, not that. "Your mother is a legend. I'd have said yes without coercion. What's the catch?"

He watches me through narrowed eyes. "Where would be the fun if I told you?"

<hr />

THROUGHOUT THE REST of the day, I can barely think about anything besides that I'm going to meet Victoria Petrov. I don't even care that most likely there's a wicked twist waiting for me. Jason is still out to get me, so there's a ninety-nine percent chance I'll be humiliated again tonight.

Jason knocks on my door at six p.m. sharp. Since I'm standing right in front of it, I know he didn't try to use his master key.

It's a miracle that I'm ready. I changed my dress a million times but ended up settling for a navy sleeveless dress with a full skirt and ballet flats. My hair color is beginning to fade, but I didn't have time to fix that. I hope she doesn't recognize me.

I have to suppress a gasp when I open the door. Jason is put together for once. No messy hair or wrinkled clothes. His dark-gray jacket fits him like a glove. He looks like a fairy-tale prince.

His gaze drops to my shoes and slowly travels back up to my face. "You look nice."

"Thanks. So do you."

Shit. Why did I say that? This isn't a date.

He quirks an eyebrow but doesn't offer a smart-ass comment.

"I'm ready. Let me get my purse," I add quickly, trying to save face.

Jason is unnaturally quiet on the way to his car. It's not until we're off to his mother's house that it occurs to me I should have driven on my own. This is looking and feeling a lot like a date, and I'm not keen. More problematic is that being trapped in the small space with him makes it impossible to escape the heady scent of his cologne. The smell is doing all sorts of crazy things to my body: stomach twisted into knots, palms sweaty, and heartbeat erratic. I don't like this cocktail of reactions.

"How come you picked the violin and not the piano?" I break the silence when I can no longer bear it.

"I sucked at the piano."

Wow. That confession came fast and unexpectedly. "Do you want to hear a secret?"

He peels his gaze off the road for a second. "Are you so mesmerized by my dashing good looks that you decided to fess up to why you killed Isabelle Maldonaro?"

I snort. "Don't flatter yourself. I'm not mesmerized by you."

"For a pathological liar, you're horrible at it."

"Never mind." I glance out the window, annoyed with myself for trying to have a civil conversation with him.

"Fine. Tell me a secret."

I should ignore him now, but that will go against my plan. In order to understand Jason's deranged mind, I must get closer to him.

"My favorite instrument is the piano, not the violin."

He doesn't reply right away, so I glance at him. He's frowning.

After another second, he flicks his gaze to mine. "So what happened? Did you suck at it too?"

I laugh without humor. "No, my parents moved a lot, and a

piano was too cumbersome. They convinced me to play a smaller instrument. I didn't want to play the violin, but when I started receiving praise from instructors and winning competitions, it grew on me. Now I can't think about playing any other instrument."

Jesus, I ended up revealing way more than I intended. Jason remains silent for a while. Curious, I glance at him. His jaw is tense, and his mouth is set in a harsh line. *Great.* I pissed him off already. It seems he hates that I'm good at playing the violin. Is it possible that he's jealous of my success?

"Basically, what you're saying is that you're an attention-seeking whore," he replies finally.

The venom in his tone hurts more than his actual words.

"We're artists. We're all attention-seeking whores. Don't you dare sit on your high horse and pretend you aren't one."

Surprisingly, he laughs. "Touché."

I refrain from talking for the rest of the trip. What Jason said bothered me and made me doubt my motivation in life. Is it possible that I care more about the fame than the art? My parents wouldn't have taken my violin from me if they didn't know I'd be tempted to perform for an audience. If I cared only about the craft, I could just play for myself.

I'm in a sour mood when he finally parks the car in front of a beachfront mansion. There's nothing unique about the building, it's just your generic modern white house with a lot of windows, super common on the expensive Southern California coast.

He gets out and strides to the front door without waiting for me. He's back to acting like a jerk, and that cements the notion this is not a date; it's a business transaction. I come to dinner with him, he doesn't pressure me about my secret for another day.

He's already inside the house when I catch up with him. The

foyer is huge with a high ceiling and a whole lot of nothing save for a grand staircase. The white walls hurt my eyes.

While I'm busy staring, Jason moves on to the outside area facing the beach.

"We're here," he announces.

I hurry to join him, feeling a little sick that I'm about to meet his mother. She's standing at the railing, looking at the ocean. The salt in the air brings good memories of when I was younger and lived in Florida. That was before we moved to Spain. I've always loved the beach. When she turns, I see the cigarette between her fingers. Her features are striking. High cheekbones, beautiful blue eyes—the same shade as Jason's—and dark hair.

"This is Nicola Devlin." Jason points at me.

The woman gives me an elevator glance, and when she's done with her inspection, I feel like I failed. There's no warmth in her gaze.

"So, this is the girl who Mrs. Simpson thought was good enough to play with you."

"The one and only." Jason sticks his hands in his pockets, attempting to look casual, but I notice the tension in his shoulders. He's hating being here.

"Hmm. I think I need to hear her play for myself to judge."

"Uh, I didn't bring my violin," I say.

"You can borrow one of Jason's. Go fetch it, boy."

Even though we're enemies, I feel bad for him. She's treating him like a dog.

His nostrils flare, but he doesn't talk back. He pivots and goes inside.

"Why did you invite me to dinner?" I ask.

"I need to know what I'm dealing with. I've given up hope that Jason will ever make waves in the classical music scene, but at least he was the best at Maverick Prep. I'd hate to see a nobody swoop in and erase all my hard work."

Jesus. This woman is vile. No wonder Jason is the way he is.

He returns a moment later holding a violin. I'm sure he heard what his mother just said. He practically shoves the instrument into my hands and then plops onto the couch. "Go on, Nicola. Dazzle us."

His attitude grates on my nerves, but my animosity toward his mother is greater. I don't want to give her more ammunition to humiliate Jason. If I play like myself, I have no doubt she'll flay him alive for not being as good as me. I've seen it plenty of times before. Parents who can't accept their child's limitations. Not everyone is a prodigy, and that should be okay. I've witnessed many of my friends have nervous breakdowns because of parental pressure.

I play for her, but I do it badly. It goes against my nature to suck this hard, but I don't need to prove myself to this witch. I'm not a show pony. Because the sound I'm making is so horrible, I keep it short.

When I lower the violin, they're both glowering.

"What the hell was that?" she asks.

I shrug. "You asked me to play, so I did."

She turns to Jason. "How bad have you gotten if Mrs. Simpson thinks this trash is at your level?"

Whoa. Things escalated fast. I didn't expect to be called names.

Jason gets up. "We're done here, Mother."

He strides back inside the house, leaving me alone with the horrible woman.

I glare at her. "You know, they're right when they say you should never meet your idol. You're a fucking disappointment."

I hurry to catch up with Jason, knowing he won't think twice before leaving me behind. He already has the engine on when I slide into the passenger seat with his damn violin in my hand.

He peels away before I have the chance to put my seat belt on. "Slow down, buddy."

He ignores me as the car keeps gaining speed. I notice after a while that we're not going back to school. He takes the scenic route, a winding road hugging the cliffs. One side is solid rock, and the other, certain death if he misses a curve.

That's it. He's going to commit suicide and take me with him. I don't talk, afraid that if I say anything, it'll distract him. Instead, I clutch the door handle and pray to survive this ride from hell.

But Jason is an expert driver, and he knows how to handle the curves. He stops when he reaches a lookout point. Jason gets out of the car and walks all the way to the edge.

I debate whether I should follow him. In the end, I do, because I'm partially to blame for his behavior. Call me a glutton for punishment, but I can't see someone suffer like this even if he's the enemy. Or maybe I like lost causes.

"Jason, are you okay?" I ask.

"Why did you do that?" he asks without looking at me.

"I didn't like her attitude. She didn't deserve my best."

He turns, and this close to the ocean and under the light of the sunset, his eyes are even more stunning. "You played like shit on purpose. Now she thinks I play like that too."

"Why do you care what she thinks?"

"Because she's Victoria fucking Petrov!"

Not because she's his mother. I begin to have a clearer picture of what his upbringing was like.

I take a step closer and touch his arm. "I don't care who she is. Her opinion shouldn't matter."

"You don't know anything," he grits out. "How could you? You've always been the best, living a perfect life. I don't fucking know why you would throw it all away."

"I wasn't the best, and my life was far from perfect. Maybe if you'd stop looking at your own navel for once, you'd be able to see that."

His eyes shine with rage, making me fear he's thinking about tossing me over the cliff.

I'm not going to wait for him to try. I turn around and stride back to the car.

"Oh no, you're not getting the last word." He grabs my arm and spins me around, pulling me flush against his body.

"Let me go, asshole."

This time I fight with everything I have. I'm too angry at myself for trying to be the bigger person. He doesn't deserve it.

Suddenly, his fingers are in my hair and his mouth slants over mine roughly. My body tenses while my brain goes haywire. *Jason Novak is kissing me.*

He pries my lips open with his tongue, and the moment it connects with mine, it's game over. I surrender to his invasion, knowing this is probably the second biggest mistake of my life. I have to hold on to his arms to remain standing, because his fiery kiss is quickly melting my body. I never knew hate could taste this good.

As sudden as it began, it ends. Jason pulls back, breathing hard. His eyes are wide, as if he can't believe what just happened. I'm still dazed, so I don't react fast enough when he returns to his car. It's not until the engine purrs to life that his intentions become clear. He takes off, leaving me stranded on the side of the road, taking my damn purse and phone with him.

Son of a bitch.

10

NICOLA / ISABELLE

I cannot believe this. Jason did leave me behind. I knew he was capable of that, but his passionate kiss threw me off. Now I'm reeling for more reasons than one. I can't tell how far I am from the Maverick campus; I'm not yet familiar with the town. There's nothing for me but to start walking. At least I know the direction I must go. There's no other way but down.

The sun quickly makes its descent and soon, darkness drops like a blanket over me. I'd like to say it doesn't bother me, but some fears are hard to conquer. The last time I was alone in the dark was when Juan was chasing me. The landscape is different, and the sound of waves crashing against the rocks below is soothing, but I can't help the spike of panic that's threatening to take control.

Damn it, Jason. I could forgive you for many things, but not this.

I don't know how long I walk, but I'm nowhere near the

bottom of the hill. The sound of an approaching vehicle makes me tense. It's coming up the mountain and, for a second, I think it's Jason. It's not until the vehicle speeds by that I see it isn't him. Disappointment rushes through me all over again.

I keep going, but then stop when I hear the car's tires screech. *Shit.* I hope that whoever's driving isn't a psycho who just spotted their next victim.

"Nicola?" a girl asks.

I turn and squint my eyes, trying to see who called me. All I see is the shape of someone's head sticking out the car window. "Who is it?"

She opens the door and gets out. "It's Sage."

I say a little prayer in my head. *Thank God.*

"What are you doing here? Did your car break down?" she asks.

"No. It's a long story. I do need a ride back to campus though."

"Yeah, sure thing. Come on."

I have no idea who's behind the wheel. I hope it's not Justice.

To my relief, it's Sage's brother, Luke. "Thanks for stopping. I have no idea how long it would take to get back to campus on foot."

"No problem. How did you end up out here?" he asks as he makes a U-turn.

"It's a long story."

"We have time."

Why is everyone so damn curious about my business? It's annoying. But I can't begrudge them the information. I do owe them big time.

"Jason left me stranded."

"*What?*" Sage asks at the same time her brother asks "Why?"

I don't want to tell them about the kiss. "To be honest, I don't know. He took me to have dinner with his mother, and that didn't go well. Then he brought me to the lookout point and bailed."

"That's horrible," Sage says. "I had no idea Jason could be so cruel."

"That's the thing though," Luke pipes up. "Jason isn't cruel unless it's warranted. Something tells me you're not telling us the whole story, *Nicola*."

"I think maybe you don't know your friend that well, *Luke*." I don't hide my annoyance.

I don't want to be ungrateful, but I'm sick and tired of people treating me badly based on assumptions. And Jason loathes me for reasons I can't fathom.

"Even if Nicola had done something to aggravate Jason, he shouldn't have left her stranded. It's not safe. She could have been run over," Sage retorts.

That possibility didn't cross my mind. I was too busy freaking out about the darkness.

The conversation dies out, and I'm left alone with my thoughts for a couple of minutes. That is until Sage breaks the silence. "I heard you're going to play at the recital. I didn't know you played the violin."

"Yeah, I dabble a little."

"I doubt that. Mrs. Simpson is super selective about the students who join her program. She must have been impressed by your talent. And she gave you a solo!"

"Not a solo. A duet with Jason."

Luke chuckles. "Oh, I can't wait to watch that performance."

"You don't like classical music," Sage replies.

"But I love catastrophe, and that duet will be explosive. Mark my words."

I want to say something to the contrary, but I can't. He's not wrong.

A cell phone rings in the car, and a moment later, Luke answers it. "Hey, Finn, what's up?"

There's a pause, and then Luke continues. "You know I don't pass up a burger from Dennis's Diner." He turns to Sage. "Wanna go out for dinner?"

"Sure." She looks over her shoulder. "Do you want to come?"

I open my mouth to say no, but Luke beats me to the punch. "She's coming. Maverick Prep is out of the way. I can drop her off after, or she can Uber home."

I'm beginning to dislike this guy. He's rude as hell.

I bite my tongue for Sage's sake. "I didn't actually have dinner, and I'm famished. Burger and fries are always a good idea."

Never mind that I don't have my wallet on me. I can pay Sage back later.

JASON

I CAN'T BELIEVE I ran away from Isabelle again. I'm a fucking coward. I just have to admit I'm fucked in the head and somehow my hatred for her has evolved into some sick physical attraction. Instead of denying it, maybe I should let it play out.

I come to that realization as soon as I see the campus buildings. And then comes the guilt. I left her alone miles and miles away in the dark and without a cell phone. I want to make her suffer, but I don't want her to actually get killed in a hit-and-run.

Jesus. I pass a hand over my face. *What the hell am I doing?* I make a U-turn and press the pedal to the metal. I try not to look too closely at my contradictory feelings. Hate, guilt, attraction. What's next? Love?

I laugh out loud. If that happens, I'll voluntarily check into a psych ward.

It hasn't been that long since I left, but when I don't find Isabelle anywhere on the way up to the lookout point, a sinking feeling hits my stomach. My worry grows exponentially. If I think logically, the most probable explanation is that she got a ride. But what if she didn't?

I hurry back to campus, and once I'm in the building, I make a beeline for her room. I knock on her door, and when she doesn't answer, I use my master key.

Her room is empty.

Hell. Where is she?

I'm not prone to panic attacks, but I think I'm having one. This isn't the first time Isabelle has messed with my emotions. When I heard she died, I had a fit of rage, and then came the depression. I couldn't understand what was happening to me. I hated her for so long that I felt cheated out of retaliation when she died. But then she came back into my life like a ghost, and the old wounds reopened. They never healed in the first place.

This would be the perfect opportunity to raid her room and find clues about her past, but I can't think about anything besides making sure she's safe.

I call Finn, the only person I can trust with this shit.

It takes a while for him to answer, and when he does, I hear loud noises in the background. "Hey, Jason. What's up?"

"I need your help."

"What's wrong?" His tone changes to match mine.

I run my fingers through my hair. "Hell, I fucked up. I left Nicola stranded near Trident Lookout Point, and now, I can't find her anywhere."

"Well, today is your lucky day, cuz. She just walked into Dennis's Diner."

"What? How did she get there that fast?"

"I'm guessing Luke and Sage gave her a lift."

A wave of relief washes over me. "Thank fuck."

"I didn't know you were dating her."

"I'm not," I grit out. "And if you value your life, don't ever repeat that out loud again."

"Sorry. Are you coming here?"

"No."

I end the call. It was rude as fuck, but there's too much going on in my head. I'll apologize to Finn later. I guess now that I know Isabelle is not in the hands of some psycho getting chopped to bits, I can raid her room without an ounce of remorse.

11

NICOLA / ISABELLE

"So, Nicola. Tell us more about yourself," Finn says, grinning in a cocky way.

Now that I know he's Jason's cousin, I can't stop seeing the similarities. They could pass for brothers.

I was afraid this would happen. Naturally, Luke had to open his big mouth and tell his friends where he found me and why.

I shrug. "There's nothing to tell. My parents have a busy work schedule, and they decided to send me to boarding school."

"Yes, but why Triton Cove? There are more exciting cities in the world," Sage chimes in.

Reid, a boy with the shaggy blond hair I met tonight, frowns. "Triton Cove isn't that bad. Look at all the tourists we get every year."

"Ignore Reid. He's a diehard fan of his hometown," Cameron interjects.

"I think it's lovely," I say, hoping we can stay on this topic and not my backstory.

Wishful thinking.

"Let's not change the subject," Finn interrupts. "I want to know why Jason is bent out of shape because of you."

"You'll have to ask him that," I retort. "Can we please talk about something else? I'm boring, folks. Trust me. Nothing exciting happens in my life. Well, until I met Jason."

Reid chuckles. "Yeah, welcome to Triton Cove."

Cameron's attention switches to a spot behind me. "Hey, isn't that Emily Frost? I haven't seen her in school yet."

Luke is now looking in her direction as well. I'm curious, so I turn. A pale girl with white-blonde hair secured in a severe ponytail is at the cashier, paying for a take-out order. She stands out. Her clothes are too mature for someone her age.

"Who is she?" I ask.

"Some weird chick who goes to Maverick," Luke replies through a scowl.

"Luke and Emily have a feud going on. It started in kindergarten," Sage tells me in a conspiratorial way.

He throws a fry at her. "We don't have a feud going on. I just don't like Bible thumpers, that's all."

"She's not a Bible thumper," Sage retorts.

"She goes to church every Sunday, and she wears those grandma clothes. Do I need to say more?"

"You're so judgmental, bro. Don't you know girls who are super repressed are the best in bed?" Cameron pipes up.

"Dude! My sister is right here," Luke complains.

Sage glowers. "What? You don't think I can handle talking about sex?"

"You shouldn't be talking or thinking about it. You're sixteen, for fuck's sake."

"You're such a hypocrite, Luke. You're only one year older than me."

He opens his mouth to reply, but I cut him off. "If you say it's different because you're a guy, I'll seriously kick you under the table."

"Ohhh," Reid and Cameron say in a teasing tone.

Finn shakes his head, and mumbles, "Oh God. Here we go again..."

I'm not sure why I'm getting such opposite reactions from Luke's friends.

He's staring at me with his mouth agape, but then he throws his head back and laughs. "Jason is so fucked."

MAYBE I GAINED brownie points with Luke after I told him what I'd do to him. All I know is that his attitude changed by the time he drove us back to Maverick Prep. He was way more relaxed, and even cracked jokes.

"See you later, Nicola. Try to not rip Jason's nutsack off. He's a good guy, even if he doesn't act like one." He smirks.

What an odd thing to say, but I reply, "I can't make any promises. Thank you for the ride. And Sage, I'll pay you back tomorrow, okay?"

"Oh, don't worry about it. See you later."

I'm feeling a little bit better after hanging out with them. And I thought tonight was going to be a total disaster. Maybe I can learn more about Jason by hanging with Finn and his friends instead of trying to get closer to him. He's like a forest of thorns. I'll get pricked if I try to explore it.

God, that sounded dirty.

My improved mood plummets to the bowels of hell when I walk into my room and find it in complete disarray. All my clothes and documents are scattered on the floor. The few books I have were opened and tossed without regard.

"That son of a bitch," I say as fury courses through my veins.

I would march up to his room right now if I knew the number. I see a pair of scissors on my desk and grab them before I walk out. I'm a possessed woman, and now, Jason will have a taste of my wrath.

I may not know where he lives, but I know where his car is parked. It's getting late and I don't bump into a lot of people. No one seems to notice the deranged glint in my eyes or the scissors in my hand. If they did, they'd surely call the police. I must look like someone who is about to commit murder.

The garage is devoid of people but full of cars. It takes me a while to find Jason's. But when I do, I go savage on his tires. I stab and slash until all four of them are in tatters. I even break a sweat, and my arms ache from the effort.

I don't care. Now we're even.

12

JASON

I didn't find anything in Isabelle's room that clued me in to why she's faking being Nicola. That pissed me off, so naturally, I took my frustration out on her room. I also returned her purse so she'd have no doubt who was the culprit. I was hoping she'd come find me to yell and fight. I was disappointed that she didn't.

My phone pings, and I know it's way too fucking early to get up. I shove my face under the pillow, then blindly reach for the device on my nightstand. I press any random button, making it stop, only for the blasted thing to start again.

"What the hell."

I grab it to shut the alarm off completely, then I see that it isn't the alarm. It's Finn calling me.

"This better be good, motherfucker, because cousin or not, I'll kick your ass for waking me up at this ungodly hour on a Saturday."

"Aren't you a ray of sunshine? Just calling to tell you, *jackass,* that your car was trashed last night."

I sit up faster than I can blink. "What?"

"Just saw it when I came in. All four tires were slashed."

Son of a *bitch.* Only one person would be insane enough to do that to me. "Thanks for letting me know."

"Do you think it was Nicola?"

"Probably."

"A bit extreme as a retaliation."

"Well, I trashed her room."

"Brutal. Do I even want to know why?"

"It's complicated. Better if you don't."

My deal with Isabelle is too fucked up. I don't need Finn to look at me as if I'm a deranged ass. I'm well aware that I am, but I'd rather not disclose that to anyone.

"All right. Just don't let the guys find out. They look up to you, and I wouldn't put it past Luke or Cam to avenge you or some shit."

"*No one* touches Nicola," I growl. "She's mine."

"Okaaay. Well, I gotta go to practice. Talk later."

I toss my phone to the side and think about what I'm going to do to Isabelle. She must have been out of her mind to exact revenge against me, knowing I can reveal her secret at any moment. Or maybe she caught on that I don't plan to do that yet.

I could make her pay right away, but it will be more satisfying to let her wait on pins and needles, wondering when my payback will come. I smile despite the vicious headache. The game just became a hundred times more interesting.

NICOLA / ISABELLE

I DID NOT SLEEP WELL last night, and it shows this morning. The dark circles under my eyes look like I've been punched. It felt great to destroy Jason's car at that moment. Now that I'm no longer controlled by rage, I'm terrified of what's going to happen next.

My stomach is twisted in a ball of dread. I expect him to storm into my room any minute. He doesn't. I check my phone. There aren't any threatening messages either. Sitting on my bed, I stare at it without moving for longer than I care to admit.

Come on, Isabelle. Snap out of it.

When I begin to feel tendrils of panic wrapping around my heart, I jump from my bed. I've done the deed; it's pointless to agonize over the consequences. It's the weekend, and my plan before the whole revenge deal happened was to do some shopping in town.

I could study, but that means staying in my room, which will result in me obsessing about Jason. So I'm sticking to my original plan. Seeing people other than the students of Maverick Prep will distract me.

Before I take a shower, I prop my chair against the door. Jason has the bad habit of barging in when I'm naked. It's like he has a sixth sense for that, or he installed a camera in my room.

I stop. *Shit.* That possibility never occurred to me before, but it fits his MO. Instead of getting ready, I search my room for hidden cameras. It takes me an hour or so to look in every corner and nook and cranny, and I don't find any.

When I glance at the time, I'm annoyed that it's already ten thirty. I wanted to head out early. Finding a parking spot downtown will be hell now.

I take a quick shower, not bothering to wash my hair, and then pick the most comfortable and understated ensemble I can find: dark jeans, a plain T-shirt, and a denim jacket paired with sneakers. It's sunny out, so I forgo the stupid contact lenses. I'll just wear sunglasses the entire time.

I was calmer during the getting ready process, but as I step outside my room, my pulse accelerates. I keep looking over my shoulder as I walk to the garage. My car is intact—I didn't really expect Jason's payback to be the same as mine.

Maybe he doesn't know yet.

I drive by where his car was parked last night and find the spot vacant. He knows. I hold the steering wheel tighter and head out. In the back of my mind, I'm aware that he can go in my room again and cause more damage, but I won't build my own cage. I've been a prisoner before, and that's not something I want to repeat. *Ever.*

My mind is spiraling during the drive. I barely notice the journey, and it's a miracle I don't get into a wreck. As predicted, I can't find a parking spot on any of the streets downtown, which forces me to park a few blocks away from the main business area. As long as I don't linger past sunset, I'll be okay.

I have no idea what I want to buy, so I visit as many shops as I can and try not to think about Jason. Unfortunately, I can't get him out of my mind. I'm afraid of him, but also intrigued by him.

You also have the hots for him, Isabelle. Let's not forget that.

My stomach grumbles, reminding me that it's late and I haven't eaten. I decide to return to the diner where we ate last night, because the food was delicious. Before I turn a corner onto Oak Street, I hear someone speaking in Spanish. The voice sounds exactly like Juan's.

My heart leaps into my throat. My entire body begins to shake, and as the voice comes closer, my survival instincts take over. I cross the street, blind to everything, while I keep chanting in my head that he's found me.

A horn blares, making me turn. The car is coming at me too

fast, and there's no chance it will stop before it hits me. Suddenly, I'm yanked out of the way onto the curb.

"Are you okay?" someone asks me.

My breathing is coming out in bursts, and my ears are ringing. I can't believe I was almost run over. I look across the street and see the guy I thought was Juan. No similarities whatsoever. I freaked out over nothing.

"It's Nicola, right?" my savior asks me again.

I finally turn to him.

It's Justice. He's so tall, I have to crane my neck to look at his face. "Yeah, thank you."

"No need to thank me. You really need to pay attention before crossing the street here. Very few people respect the speed limit."

"I know."

He releases my arm but keeps his attention on me. "You look pale. Are you sure you're okay?"

"I'm a little shaken. I was heading to Dennis's Diner for lunch."

"What a coincidence. So was I. Are you meeting anyone there?"

"No, I'm flying solo today. You?"

"I have to meet someone later, so I was just going to kill time there. Maybe we can hang out."

Would it look bad if I ate lunch with Justice? I'm not interested in him, and I know Jason doesn't like him. But hell, the guy just saved my life and saying no would be rude. Besides, I shouldn't care what that jerk thinks.

"Yeah, let's."

I feel better having company now. I don't know Justice, but he seems all right. He opens the door and urges me to walk in first. The place is full, so we wait for the hostess.

This time, a cute redheaded teen greets us. She smiles at me, but when she turns her attention to Justice, her grin wilts a fraction. Does she know him?

"Welcome to Dennis's Diner," she says.

"Hi, Alexis. Long time," Justice replies.

"Yeah. Follow me."

Okay, I'm definitely not imagining things. Our waitress knows Justice and doesn't like him very much.

Once we're seated, she asks, "What can I get you to drink?"

"Just water for me," I say.

"Same," Justice adds.

"All right. I'll be right back."

Once she's out of earshot, I ask him, "Where do you know her from?"

"We went to middle school together. Alexis's dad owns the diner."

"She wasn't very friendly toward you," I point out.

He leans back and shrugs. "I dated her best friend for a couple of months, and when I broke things off, I became the villain. You know, the usual."

I frown. "It's not usual unless you did something to warrant a bad reputation."

He squints and then smiles. "Nah, I swear I did nothing to Carmen. I just didn't like her as a girlfriend."

A moment later, Alexis returns with our drinks.

"Did you make your choice, or do you need a couple more minutes?" she asks.

I open the menu to search for the item that caught my eye yesterday. "I'll try the Dennis Super Charged Dog. It sounds delicious."

"Oh yeah, it's one of my favorites," she replies with a smile.

"I'll have the usual." Justice grins at her, but his smile has no warmth.

"Right." Her expression closes off as she jots something down on her pad. "The food shouldn't take long."

The exchange between them leaves something foul lingering

in the air. Luke told Sage he didn't like Justice because he was shady, and I'm beginning to wonder if he was right.

"So, Nicola, tell me what brought you to Triton Cove."

I repeat the rehearsed story, but Justice keeps looking at his phone. I could have told him the truth and he wouldn't have batted an eyelash.

"Are you from Triton Cove?" I ask to get the ball into his court.

"No, I moved here when I was twelve."

"How did you end up at Maverick Prep?"

"I got a basketball scholarship. I wouldn't be able to afford the tuition otherwise."

I raise my brows. "That's cool."

Alexis returns with our food, and I'm glad for the interruption. The sooner we eat, the sooner this strange hangout can end.

I get distracted by the food and manage to ignore my companion while I eat.

He laughs. "Wow."

I lift my face. "What?"

"I've never seen a girl destroy a Dennis Super Charged Dog that fast."

I shrug. "I'm motivated when I'm hungry."

He lifts his hand, and before I can react, he wipes the corner of my mouth with his thumb. My spine becomes rigid in an instant. *Boundaries, dude.*

"You had mustard on your face," he says.

I reach for a napkin and wipe my mouth before he finds another smear that he feels he needs to clean with his fingers.

"Justice?" a familiar voice calls him.

His eyes widen in a guilty way. "Hey, Sage. How is it going?"

Shit. Did she see her crush getting frisky with me? I turn with a smile ready, but seeing her cold expression answers the question for me. She did see Justice touch my face.

"Hi, Sage," I say.

"Hi." Her tone is cold, matching her hard stare.

Without another word, she pivots and walks out. Justice scrambles to his feet and rushes after her. *Damn it.* There's something going on between them, and now that I've hung out with the guy, I agree with Luke. He's bad news.

I stare at my half-eaten hot dog, knowing I won't finish it. I lost my appetite.

"Did Justice just ditch you?" Alexis asks.

I didn't even notice her approach. "Uh, this wasn't a date. We bumped into each other and realized we were both coming here for lunch."

Her eyebrows arch. "Oh. Well, you looked pretty chummy for a moment." She shakes her head. "I'm sorry. It's none of my business."

"You don't like him very much, do you?"

"Nope. I'd be careful if I were you."

It's not me I'm worried about. I look out the window, but I don't see Justice or Sage anywhere. "Thanks for the heads-up. Can I have the bill, please?"

She flicks her gaze to Justice's unfinished burger. "Are you covering his share too?"

"Yeah, might as well. If he comes back, tell him he's all set."

"If he doesn't return before you're gone, his food goes in the trash. We're too busy—we need the table."

"Right." I nod.

I have a feeling that even if the diner wasn't busy, she'd toss his food in the garbage. He doesn't return before I head out, and I begin to worry about Sage. I send her a quick text, but it goes unanswered.

Crap. I don't want her to think there's something going on between Justice and me. Maybe I should tell her brother what happened today, but she might be even more upset if I rat her out.

I'm still thinking about what to do when my phone pings. I look at it, hoping it's Sage, but it's a text from the bane of my existence.

JASON: I guess you *do* like pervs.

HELL, how did he find out about Justice so quickly?

13

NICOLA / ISABELLE

*W*hen I got home on Saturday, I called Sage. She ignored it and never called me back. So I sent her a long text message explaining how I wound up in the diner with Justice. I know that if she saw the guy touching my face, it looked bad. And God knows what he told her.

Jason didn't bother me again. I decided it was best to stay in my room on Sunday and study, but my mind wasn't into it. As weekends go, this one sucked.

I look like a raccoon today. It takes me longer than usual to get ready, so I don't have time for breakfast. I don't think I could eat anyway.

My nerves are shot as I walk into the school building. I barely make it into the main hallway when Sloane and her friends block my path.

I don't need this shit today.

"Excuse me," I say.

"No, I won't excuse you." Sloane flattens one hand on my shoulder and shoves me against a locker.

"Hey! Get off me."

"This is your first and last warning. Stay away from Jason."

I should have predicted Sloane would show her claws. When I met Jason, she clearly made a show for my benefit. All that was left was for her to piss all over him to mark her territory.

"Why? Because you have some sick claim over him?"

Her face twists into a scowl. "You're the one who's the oddity here, bitch."

I could tell her I have no interest in Jason, and he's the one who won't leave me alone. But she wouldn't believe me, and hell, I don't owe her any explanation.

But I won't take her threats meekly. I shove her off me, hard. She staggers back as her eyes grow larger.

Didn't expect the weirdo to fight back, did you, bitch?

"What's the meaning of this?" the principal asks, scowling in my direction.

Great. He has to show up when I'm defending myself. I bet he didn't see Sloane shove me against the locker first.

"I don't know, Mr. Cain. This girl is a menace. We just wanted to know where she bought her shoes," Sloane replies, milking the fake sweet tone to the max.

Her friends all jump in to confirm her BS story.

"Nicola, please follow me," he says.

Damn everything to hell.

I do as he says, but I make sure to glare at Sloane as I walk by her. She's smirking, and I want nothing more than to wipe that smug smile off her face.

When I'm alone with him, the headmaster looks pissed, even more so than he did in the hallway. The door is closed, and his assistant can't hear anything.

"I'm very disappointed in your behavior, Isabelle."

Hearing him call me by my real name makes me cringe.

"Isabelle is dead. I'd prefer it if you called me Nicola," I grit out.

He folds his hands on the desk and leans forward. "Very well, *Nicola*. Your parents went through a lot of trouble to get this second chance for you. I'd hate to see you squander it with pettiness."

"I was defending myself," I say through clenched teeth. "I didn't realize you condoned bullying at Maverick Prep."

"I don't. I didn't ask you to follow me here because of what I witnessed just a moment ago."

"Oh? Why am I here, then?"

"We have footage of you vandalizing Jason Novak's car on Friday night."

My stomach bottoms out. The altercation with Sloane made me forget about my problems with Jason.

"He deserved it. He trashed my room."

His eyebrows shoot up. "And do you have proof that he did that?"

"No, but I know it was him. He has a master key."

Mr. Cain laughs. "There isn't a master key to any room in the dorms, Ms. Devlin."

I don't know if he's lying to save face or if Jason lied about his master key. It doesn't matter, though. I can't *prove* that he messed with me first.

I cross my arms. "He has a key to *my* room."

"If that's the case, we can easily change the lock. But I'm afraid I can't ignore the fact you destroyed his car."

The sinking feeling in the pit of my stomach intensifies. "What does that mean? Am I suspended?"

"No. It turns out Jason spoke on your behalf."

My heart skips a beat, and then it accelerates to a hundred. "He did?"

"Yes. He made me aware you have a recital coming soon, and that you must practice until then. It's for that reason, and that reason alone, that you're not getting a suspension. But I advise you to work out your issues with other students in a less destructive manner."

"I'll try."

"No, Ms. Devlin. Don't try. Simply do. You can head to class now."

My mind is spinning like a top as I head to Spanish. I wish I could believe that Jason interceded on my behalf because there's something good in him. But the most logical explanation is that he wants to deal with me in his own twisted way.

I spot him ahead of me in the hallway, talking to Sloane. They look chummy, which causes an ugly feeling to spread through my chest. I can't possibly be jealous of him and that bitch. I should look away, but I don't before Jason turns his head in my direction. Our eyes lock. I can't glance away first. I don't want him to think I'm afraid of him. He smirks before he returns his attention to Sloane.

He tucks a strand of her hair behind her ear and then kisses her cheek. I don't know if he's doing that because I'm watching or not.

Look away, Isabelle.

I don't and end up bumping into someone.

"Hey, wat—" Luke starts before he sees me. "Oh, it's you."

"Sorry. I was distracted."

His gaze travels past my head. "I can see why. I wouldn't worry though. Sloane has been after Jason since I can remember. If he wanted to date her, he would have already."

"Why are you telling me? I don't care who he dates."

He smiles knowingly. "Sure you don't. Anyway, gotta go."

It doesn't occur to me until he leaves that he's acting as if he doesn't know that I hung out with Justice on Saturday. I'm sure if he knew, he wouldn't be friendly toward me. How did Jason find out about it so fast?

Like a dumbass, I look again in his direction, but he's gone.

14

NICOLA / ISABELLE

*J*ason misses Spanish, and of course I wonder if he went somewhere with Sloane. The idea irritates me beyond reason. The silver lining on the situation is that, because I'm obsessing about Jason, I don't have another panic attack in class.

During the rest of the day, I keep looking over my shoulder, waiting for Jason to spring up from a corner and do something nasty. He doesn't, and I don't get a glimpse of him anywhere until it's time for music with Mrs. Simpson.

My excitement is diminished severely knowing that I have to play with him. And worst of all, my attempt to find a violin online yesterday was an epic failure, so all I have is the ridiculous rainbow explosion Jason got me. I can already picture the mocking looks I'll get from Sloane.

I wonder what she'd do if she knew Jason kissed me on

Friday. I don't think she'd be happy, even if she also knew he abandoned me soon after.

Ah hell, why did I think about that kiss when I'm a second away from stepping into Mrs. Simpson's class?

I find Jason sitting next to Sloane and, once again, I feel a twinge of jealousy. *Fuck.* These stupid ass reactions must stop. I'm getting all bent out of shape because of one kiss? I confess, it was hot, but everything that happened after should have reset my brain to when I met him.

Jason is a jerk who's determined to make my life miserable. I shouldn't care that his kiss set me ablaze.

"Ah, good afternoon, Ms. Devlin," Mrs. Simpson says. "I see that you got your instrument."

"I got a violin, but it's definitely not *my* instrument."

"Oh?" She raises an eyebrow.

I make a show of taking the colorful violin out. "A gift from Jason. I didn't know he had a sense of humor."

Her jaw drops. "Well, that's something, for sure."

"The sound is crap, but I can make do until I buy a proper violin," I continue.

"I'm sure you can. Well, take a seat and let's commence."

I'm happy that I manage to cross the classroom without looking in Jason's direction. But I can feel his hard stare burning a hole through my face. Is he angry that I didn't acknowledge his presence, or that I told Mrs. Simpson I'd buy a new violin?

God, why do I care?

During most of the lesson we practice one piece as a group. It's not until there are only ten minutes left in class that Mrs. Simpson discusses my duet with Jason. She wants us to play Tchaikovsky's *Romeo and Juliet Fantasy Overture* because it's powerful and romantic. I don't know why she thinks that's a good idea. Plus, there isn't a duet in that piece, only a solo. If Tchaikovsky wanted the solo to be a duet, he would have composed it as such. It's official, the woman is insane.

Standing now in the middle of the room with Jason, it's impossible to not look at him. His gaze is dark as he listens to Mrs. Simpson explain her idea to us. Is he hating her choice as much as I am? I don't have time to figure out his thoughts, because the bell rings, ending the class. I have to hurry to get to my next one, since it's on the other side of the building.

I'm putting my things away hastily when Jason steps next to me.

"We need to practice, or we'll crash and burn," he tells me.

"And we can't have that, can we? What will your mother say?"

He narrows his eyes. "Careful, Nicola. Don't get cocky now."

"I'm not being cocky. I'm just making an observation."

"Be back here in an hour," he tells me.

I put my hands on my hips. "What makes you think I don't have plans in an hour?"

He smiles darkly. "I know your schedule."

"I still need to buy a proper violin."

He steps into my personal space. "I already said you'll use the violin I gave you."

My pulse accelerates at his proximity. His intoxicating aftershave reaches my nose, and my brain floods with the memory of our kiss. His stormy eyes drop to my mouth, making me suspect that he's thinking about the same thing.

"Is that how you plan to sabotage me? Are you that afraid that everyone will know I'm better than you?"

He lifts his gaze to mine again. "You're not better than me."

"I think I am. I'll wait to judge when we practice later," I reply sweetly.

His nostrils flare, reminding me that he's prone to losing control.

"Jason, what are you doing wasting your time with that loser?" Sloane interrupts.

He schools his expression into the arrogant mask he likes to wear, and steps back. "I was just making sure she understands her assignment."

"Whatever, I'm hungry. Let's go eat off campus."

Gag me. Just watching them talk is twisting my stomach. I look at the time and curse in my head. I'm going to be late if I don't hurry. I shove all my notes into my bag and then rush out of the classroom. Jason calls my name—my real name—in front of Sloane. I know he made a mistake, but if I answer, I'll give my secret away. The best course of action is to ignore him and pray she doesn't connect the dots.

JASON

I SEE Isabelle drop something from her bag, and on reflex, I call her by her real name. *Shit.* She's done something to me, because I'm not prone to making rookie mistakes like that.

"Who is Isabelle?" Sloane asks.

"I don't know." I bend over to grab what Isabelle dropped. It's her eyedrop bottle. I pocket it before Sloane can see what I got.

"You called Nicola 'Isabelle.'" Sloane is watching me through narrowed eyes now.

"Did I? I didn't notice."

She crosses her arms. "I wasn't born yesterday, Jason. Who the fuck is Isabelle? You wouldn't have called that weirdo by another name if she wasn't someone you're thinking about."

"You're under the impression I owe you an explanation. You're not my girlfriend, Sloane. You're not even my fuck buddy." I hoist my violin case over my shoulder and head out.

"You're an ass, Jason."

I ignore her. I don't have time to deal with Sloane's jealousy bullshit. It's her problem that she got it into her head that she had a chance with me.

Dating and all the annoyances attached to it were never something I was interested in. Hookups are much easier. I chose to hang out with Sloane because she wasn't boring, but now she's getting on my nerves. Sure, I've been leading her on since Isabelle walked into my life, but that strategy is giving me more headaches than it's worth.

I shove my hand in my jacket pocket and curl my fingers around the eyedrop bottle. Isabelle will miss this, and she'll have to endure dry eyes for the rest of the day or take off those hideous lenses. It's a shame she has to hide her eye color. It's gorgeous.

Jesus. I'm losing my mind. This physical attraction is getting out of hand. I can't let it distract me. It's thanks to her that my life has been a shitfest. Maybe I need to fuck her already and move on.

The twitch in my pants confirms that my cock is one hundred percent on board with the idea.

15

JASON

I'm late on purpose. It's a test to gauge Isabelle's fear of me. I haven't punished her yet for what she did to my car, and her sassiness shows she's gaining confidence. My slip of the tongue earlier in front of Sloane didn't help my case. And what's the deal with her and Justice—what was she doing with that asshole? It was by chance that I saw them together while I was out on Saturday.

I hear music from the hallway, and as much as I hate to admit it, it speaks to my soul. The violin is not the best, but she somehow has managed to make it work for her. I stand outside and listen to her play for a minute before I walk into the classroom. Her back is to me, so she doesn't notice me right away.

There's no denying it. Anyone who listens to her play will know she's in a different league than me. Old memories come to the surface. The humiliation of sucking terribly at the

84

competition, and then my mother's hateful words afterward. They were worse than my father's blows.

Before I know what I'm doing, I'm striding in her direction. She turns when I'm already practically on top of her.

"Jason, wh—"

I cover her mouth with my hand and push her back until she meets the wall.

"You've been behaving badly for someone with so much to lose, Isabelle. You didn't think I'd let your little act of vandalism go unpunished, did you?"

Her eyes widen. I remove my hand from her face, dying to hear her reply.

"You got what you deserved. You trashed my room."

My eyes narrow to slits. "You still don't get it. I can do whatever I please with your room... and with you."

"Why would I continue to play along with your games when you just blurted out my real name in front of your girlfriend? You clearly don't give a shit about keeping my secret."

I smirk to hide that I fucked up. "That was by design, darling. I wanted to remind you how easily I can expose you."

"How long are you going to keep this up?"

"For as long as it's fun. So let's make sure you don't bore me." I trace my thumb over her lips, dying for another taste.

She trembles under my caress, and I almost succumb and kiss her again. But that's not a punishment when I can see she wants me to do it.

I step away. "Take off your stupid lenses. I hate them."

"No one is forcing you to look into my eyes," she retorts.

God, even cornered, she won't back down. I don't see myself ever getting tired of toying with her.

"I only told Sloane your first name, but that was already enough to make her suspicious. Maybe next time, I'll let your last name slip."

She swallows hard, and it's audible. "If she learns who I am, you won't have leverage over me anymore."

"True, but if I don't get what I want, there's no point in keeping your secret, is there?"

She clamps her jaw shut and glowers for a moment. Then she walks around me and takes the lens case out of her bag. I watch in silence as she keeps searching for the eyedrop bottle currently in my pocket.

"Shit," she mumbles to herself.

Keeping her back to me, she removes her lenses and then turns around with her chin raised. Her eyes are red, but she still looks at me in defiance.

Let's change that.

"Are you ready to practice or what?" she asks.

"Not so fast. You need to pay for the damage to my car."

She narrows her eyes. "Are you going to ask me to strip naked and play for you again?"

"Tempting, but I want something better." I walk over, loving how she tenses at my proximity.

"I'm not going to have sex with you," she grits out.

"Oh, you will, eventually. But not today. On your knees."

Her pretty eyes widen. Then she shakes her head. "I'm not going to suck your dick either."

My fingers are in her hair in an instant, twisting a strand viciously until she winces. "You should have thought about that before you slashed my tires."

Her eyes well up with tears, almost making me feel guilty. Before I cave to the emotion, I crush my lips to hers, kissing her deep and hard. I let the anger and desire consume me, and when I sense her melting into me, I yank her head back.

"On your knees. *Now.* I'm not going to repeat it again."

"And if I don't, you'll tell everyone who I am?"

"That, or something worse."

A strange emotion flashes in her eyes, and now I want to

know what she's thinking. Is she developing a sick attraction to me like I am to her?

"Aren't you afraid I'm going to bite?" she asks.

"I know you won't, because deep down, you want this."

NICOLA / ISABELLE

I FREEZE AT HIS WORDS. Denial is on the tip of my tongue, but it'd be a lie. I'm that messed up in the head that the more Jason punishes me, the more I want him to show me his worst. I never thought I craved this type of depraved dynamic until I met him.

Juan was a sick monster. He treated me like a princess until he decided to lock me in a cage. Jason is a broken boy pretending to be a monster. He's hateful, but his cruelty is almost innocent.

God, what the hell are you thinking, Isabelle? He just ordered you to blow him in a classroom.

My lips still tingle from his brutal kiss. I can't say I don't want more. He knows he can play me any way he likes, and I'm sure he believes I'll fight him. I bet he's counting on it.

So I drop to my knees, determined to give him the best blow job of his life.

Holding his stare, I unbutton his pants and lower the zipper. His face is a cold mask, but his breathing is already different, shallower. I pull his pants down just enough to have access to his briefs. The bulk there is undeniable. I rub the fabric over his shaft, making him hiss.

"Quit stalling," he grumbles.

"I'm not. But if I'm paying a debt, I want to make sure I don't owe you anything after."

He reaches for my hair again and yanks at the strands. The pain sends a shiver of pleasure down my spine. Can he tell how turned on I am? Does he care? Or would he prefer it if I was not on board with this?

I try to read the truth in his eyes. They aren't as hard as before. Desire has clouded the hate, but I don't see malice.

"Your debt to me will never be paid, Isabelle. *Never.*"

That's where you're wrong, Jason. I just have to survive one more year of high school, and then I'll be gone.

I swallow any remark I might have made. Instead, I free his cock from his briefs and bring it to my mouth. It's bigger than I expected, but I swallow the whole thing until the head hits the back of my throat. Jason's expression softens, but his hand is firmly twisted around my hair.

"That's a good girl," he says.

I use my hand and tongue to work him, knowing that I'm doing it right when he grows larger. He lets me have control for only a minute or so before he sets the pace and fucks my mouth hard. My eyes sting from it, and a few times, he almost chokes me with his cock. I don't complain though, and when he finishes, I swallow every drop.

Breathing hard, he staggers back, zipping up his pants. Then he turns around and pulls his hair back. "Fuck."

My knees hurt from staying in this position for so long. I won't give him the satisfaction of seeing that. I get up and then grab my violin.

"Now that you had your fun, can we practice?"

He looks over his shoulder with eyes narrowed. "Who says I had any fun?"

I wipe the corner of my mouth, and then lick my finger. "This tells me you did."

16

NICOLA / ISABELLE

*W*hen I didn't think Jason's mind games could get any worse, the morning after I gave him a blow job, he emails me a video of my performance. The subject reads "Something to remember me by."

The footage doesn't show my face. The security camera I didn't know the music room had was behind me. But my colorful violin is in plain view, and there aren't many girls at Maverick Prep who have black hair like mine.

My phone rings a moment later, showing an unknown number. I never answer those calls, but on a hunch, I press the green button.

"Hello?"

"Good morning, darling," Jason drawls. "Did you get my email?"

"You're a sick fuck, aren't you? How did you get your hand on that security footage?"

He laughs. "Easy peasy when you're me."

"So you're adding that to your arsenal of blackmail?"

"Hmm, maybe."

My shoulders slump. I can't help the feeling of defeat that takes over me. I haven't ugly cried in a long time, but I think I'll break that streak this morning.

"What did I ever do to you?" I ask, hating how shaky my voice sounds.

"Oh, Isabelle. Are you crying?"

"You know what, Jason? Do what you want with that video." I end the call then turn off my phone.

I should start getting ready, but instead, I lie down in bed and bury myself under the covers. I'm so tired of it all. Whenever I think I'm getting ahead of Jason's twisted game, he comes back with something more awful to torment me.

In hindsight, people already think I'm a weirdo, what's adding whore to the mix going to do to me? Maybe I'm overreacting. I don't know. I miss my parents, my friends, and my home. To sum everything up, I miss my old life.

Sometimes I think that I should let Juan find me so we can end it once and for all. Either he kills me, or I kill him. It's better than living in suspended animation. But knowing how my last chapter with him ended, I can see how the story will go, with me dead and my body never to be found. Knowing Juan, he'd make sure I suffer. But then, I'd be free of him.

Jesus, I'm seriously depressed if I think that's a good outcome.

At some point, I fall asleep and miss class. When I wake up, I feel sluggish, and every muscle in my body hurts. The mattress dips behind me, and that's when I realize I'm not alone.

My brain must still be fuzzy, because I close my eyes and whimper, "Please, Juan, don't hurt me."

A hand on my shoulder forces me to roll on my back. It isn't Juan's face that I see hovering over mine. It's Jason's.

"Who's Juan?"

I blink fast, trying to come up with an excuse, but I can't make my brain work. "No one."

He furrows his brows, then places a hand over my forehead. "You're burning up."

I have a fever. No wonder I can't think straight.

"How did you get in here? I propped the chair against the door."

"No, you didn't. I guess you forgot, or you wanted me to come in."

I sigh. "If you're here wanting another blow job. I can't promise it'll be any good."

"I'm not that demented," he grumbles.

"Why are you in my room, then?"

"You missed class and practice. Mrs. Simpson was worried."

Yeah, it makes sense. Jason must have come here to make sure his favorite punching bag was still alive.

"If I'm too sick to practice, you'll get your solo back. Everyone will be happy."

"You're definitely sick or you wouldn't be talking nonsense."

"Just let me be, Jason."

He stands and walks to my bathroom. "Where do you keep your painkillers?"

Wait. He wants to help me?

"Never mind. I found them."

He returns to the room with a full glass of water and the pills. I lean on my elbows, trying to sit up. I don't move fast enough, and Jason ends up assisting me.

"Take two and drink the whole thing. You need to hydrate."

"Why are you helping me? Did I suck you that good yesterday?"

His eyebrows arch. "I had no idea you had such a filthy mind."

I swallow the pills with the help of the water, but I only take one sip and earn a hard stare from him.

"I said drink the whole glass."

"Stop bossing me around," I retort but do as he says.

"Good girl." He smirks.

I can't tell if I'm blushing or not, because I have a fever, but my mind automatically goes to that memory.

"You didn't answer my question. Are you helping me because you liked the way I sucked your dick, and you want a repeat?"

The amusement vanishes from his eyes. "I'm helping you because I don't want to win the solo by default."

I flop on the bed again. "Fine. Don't answer, then. I know you enjoyed yourself."

He joins me in bed, straddling me. I'm too weak to have a proper reaction to it.

"I'm a guy and I came in your mouth. Of course I enjoyed myself."

"At least one of us did."

He smirks. "I don't know why you keep lying to me. You have the worst poker face."

"I'm not lying."

His eyebrows twitch and then a smug grin unfurls on his lips. "What are you saying, Isabelle? Do you want me to get you off?"

My pulse accelerates and a crazy yearning hits me hard. *What the actual fuck?* Even burning with fever, I'm craving this asshole. Or maybe it's because my brain can't function properly that my body is taking control.

"No, I don't. What I want is for you to leave me alone."

He shakes his head. "Can't now. You know, I haven't been able to forget your sweet pussy since you played for me naked. I think I need to take a closer look."

My damn heart slams hard against my rib cage, I'm afraid it's going to burst through. I'm so turned on, that my clit is throbbing in anticipation.

I haven't had sex since Juan. There has been no time between hospital stays and fleeing my old life. But I didn't expect to be attracted to anyone else for a very long time. Juan didn't rape me, but there are worse things that can happen to a person.

Jason tosses the cover aside and then slowly peels off my pajama pants and underwear. Jesus, this is really happening.

"You said you weren't that demented to want to sex me up while I'm sick."

"And you believed me? You shouldn't have lied to me, Isabelle. Don't you know by now that it turns me on more than anything else?"

I swallow hard, not knowing what to do. I'm exposed to him from the waist down. A guy who has humiliated me time and time again, and yet, I'm not embarrassed or feeling violated. I'm oddly excited to see how this will go.

"I hate that you're so damn beautiful," he confesses.

"The feeling is mutual."

He quirks an eyebrow. "Touch yourself."

"What?" I squeak.

"You heard me. I want to see your fingers glide between your folds. I want to watch you pleasure yourself, knowing you're thinking about me."

"You are one cocky son of a bitch. You can't control my fantasies, Jason."

"Touch yourself, Isabelle," he grits out.

I bring my fingers to my mouth to lick them first before running them down my belly. Jason's eyes bug out, and I want to laugh like a delirious woman. It's amusing that he's surprised I always bring his requests up a notch.

I part my legs a little, wanting him to get a good view before I flick my clit. My hips buck unexpectedly. I wasn't prepared for the pleasure of a simple touch. I've never had this reaction to my own hand. Jason is the reason.

"You like that, don't you, my filthy liar?" he purrs.

"Yes," I hiss.

"Keep moving those fingers, darling."

I flick my clit a few more times, already sensing the tension buildup. As crazy as it sounds, I don't want to come too quickly, so I stop touching my clit in favor of teasing my entrance. Jason's pants clearly show a bulge already. I picture him taking his cock out and fucking me hard. My fingers glide inside of me, forcing me to close my eyes. It feels too damn good already.

Jason's hands find my breasts, and I let out a gasp. He keeps his expression closed off as he plays with them through my shirt. I move my fingers in and out faster, knowing I can't stop the orgasm now even if I wanted to.

Out of the blue, he grabs my wrist and yanks my hand away from my pussy.

"What are—"

He leans closer. "I'm not letting you come just yet, sweetheart. First, you need to tell me who the fuck Juan is."

17

JASON

a s mindfuck games go, this is the most demented one I've ever played with anyone. What was I thinking when I ordered Isabelle to masturbate in front of me? I'm so hard, I'm seriously risking jizzing in my pants. I'm also on the verge of replacing her fingers with my tongue. There's no doubt in my mind that she tastes fucking delicious.

But I can't give her any advantage. I grab her wrist and yank her hand from between her legs.

"What are—"

I lean closer, not caring that I might catch her cold.

"I'm not letting you come just yet, sweetheart. First, you need to tell me who the fuck Juan is."

Her white face becomes even paler, and her beautiful violet eyes grow larger.

"He's… nobody." She turns her face, and her bangs part to the side with the movement.

I see it then, the scar near her hairline. I brush the strands off to have a closer look. She bats my hand away and fixes her hair so the scar is covered again.

"How did you get that?"

"None of your business."

Pissed now that she's back at thinking she has any leverage here, I cup her pussy with my hand, making her arch her back. She's still turned on, despite the change in dynamics.

"Did Juan give you that scar, Isabelle?"

"No."

"You're lying." I plunge two fingers inside her, hard. She's so wet, they glide in easily.

"Are you going to finger me until I confess?"

"Yes. I'm going to bring you to the edge, but I won't let you take the plunge unless you tell me everything."

She closes her eyes and whimpers. I keep my fingers in place, buried deep inside her pussy, while I press my thumb over her clit. She gasps loudly.

"Is Juan the reason you faked your death, Isabelle? Tell me."

Her eyes fly open, and then she shoves me with more strength than I expected. I slide off to the side, allowing her to jump out of bed. I'm stunned, not angry. I wait for the rage to erupt from the pit of my stomach, and when it doesn't, I suspect I might be getting sick too.

She only manages a couple of steps before she collapses on the floor and covers her face with her hands. She's shaking terribly now.

Shit, I think I broke her. Too soon.

I follow her and then crouch by her side. "Isabelle?"

She turns to me, and glowers. "Yes, Juan is the reason I'm here, pretending to be someone I'm not."

My chest is tight; I'm not elated as I thought I'd be. I finally pushed her to the point of despair, but I feel wretched, not vindicated.

"What did he do?" I ask.

"You're a smart guy, Jason. What do you think? He killed me."

Her words feel like a punch to my stomach. Some motherfucker tried to take her away from me, and for a while, I thought she was truly dead. The possessiveness I felt earlier when Finn mentioned that Luke or Cameron might want to do something to Isabelle returns with a vengeance.

I pull her into a hug, not knowing if it's for her benefit or mine.

"What happened to him?" I ask in a low tone.

"Nothing. His family is too powerful. He left me for dead, and then we let him believe he succeeded."

"Tell me everything, Isabelle. I want to know *everything*."

She pulls away from me. "Why? So you can tell him where to find me?"

I capture her face between my hands. "No, so I can make sure he never hurts you again."

Her eyebrows furrow. "Oh, so you're the only one who can hurt me now. Is that it?"

"Yes." I claim her lips before she can nudge another question in.

I'm not sure what I'm doing. The rules of my own game have changed, and I don't know how to play it anymore. All I know is that I want Isabelle with as much fervor as I loathe her. There's a fine line between hate and lust, and we're past toying with it. It's now blurred beyond recognition.

She kisses me back as if she wants to drown in me. Her hands find my shoulders, and her fingers dig in. I push her back until she's lying on the floor and I'm between her legs. Her wet pussy rubs against my erection through my pants, driving me insane with need. I release her lips to place hungry kisses on her chin and down her neck. My hands are everywhere; I'm torn about what I want to explore first. I'm acting like a virgin who doesn't know what he's doing.

I lean back to take my shirt off. Then I reach for Isabelle's pajama top and rip the fabric down the middle. Like a starved man, I pounce, sucking one of her nipples into my mouth hard while my hand reaches between her legs. She moans softly, and I guess she's beyond words. So am I.

Her fingers are in my hair now, pulling at the strands. Mine are soaking wet, diving into her folds. If I keep at it, I'm going to explode in my briefs. I can't let that happen. In a frenzy, I unzip my pants and free myself. It wasn't the plan to fuck her so soon, but this will end in catastrophe one way or another, I might as well enjoy her while she'll have me.

I lift her leg, resting it over my shoulder, and then I plunge into her hard. She cries out, throwing her head back with her eyes closed.

"Look at me when I fuck you, Isabelle."

She does, and her eyes are like a purple storm. "You're one sick bastard."

I grab her by the neck and squeeze just enough to show her who's the boss. "I know, and you love it."

"I don't."

I pull back almost completely only to slam back again rougher than before. "The more you lie, the harder I get, darling."

She becomes tighter around me, making it impossible to maintain control. I don't want it to end, because she feels so fucking good. I move faster though, chasing the inevitable. Her hips buck as she climaxes first. She doesn't scream or curse my name. Instead, she bites her lower lip and closes her eyes. Her cheeks become pink, and that's my undoing. I come hard, and unlike her, I don't keep it quiet. I groan savagely as I empty myself inside her heat.

A second before I'm completely spent, I lower my mouth to hers and kiss her tenderly for the first time. I'm surprised she not only lets me, but she cups my face. I don't want to enjoy her caress, but I don't stop her from doing it either.

18

NICOLA / ISABELLE

I wake up and nothing makes sense. My brain is fuzzy as hell and shows no signs that it'll get out of this daze. I'm in bed alone. Did I hallucinate that Jason was in my room yesterday and that we had sex?

I'm wearing underwear and a long shirt, so maybe it was just a dream. I roll over to look at the spot on the floor where Jason possibly fucked me. My ripped pajama top is there, torn in two pieces. *Shit.* It did happen. I touch myself and find the area tender.

"I can't believe this."

I throw my legs over the side of the bed and sit up. I'm so confused, I don't know what to do or think anymore. Resting my elbows on my thighs, I hide my face in my hands. Sleeping with the enemy is the most fucked-up thing I've ever done. I wasn't so feverish that I didn't know what was happening. I wanted him, and hell, I still do.

Jason's mood swings make him unpredictable. One moment

he treats me like he hates me, in the next, he seems to care about my well-being. Because of a glimpse of his kindness, I told him about Juan. I was tired of keeping that secret, but now I fear I only gave Jason more power over me.

I trudge to the bathroom and barely glance at my reflection in the mirror before I jump into the shower. I don't feel as awful as I did yesterday. My body could use more rest, but not knowing what Jason is up to will raise my anxiety through the roof.

I'm too tired to bother with my contact lenses today. Let everyone believe my natural eye color is fake. My hair is already almost back to its natural light-brown color, so going without the brown lenses is a risk. It seems now that Jason knows my secret, I'm less paranoid about others finding out. What are the chances that another student here knows who I am? He recognized me only because of who his mother is.

I leave for breakfast, but I don't make it outside the building before my cell phone rings. I check the call, and it's the same unsaved number as before. Only now I know it's Jason's.

"What do you want? It's too early for your games."

"I'm dying," he replies in a raspy voice. "All thanks to you."

"Wait. Are you sick too?"

"No, I like impersonating Don Corleone."

I pinch the bridge of my nose. "I'm sorry you caught my cold. But why are you calling me?"

"Because everything hurts, and I don't want anyone to see me like this."

"But you don't care if I do?"

There's a pause, and then he replies, "I guess I don't."

I'm about to ask what he needs, but I stop myself. Why would I help Jason without asking for anything in return? He's giving me an opportunity here, and I'd be a fool not to take it.

"Let me get this straight—are you asking for my help?"

"I'm asking you to fix what you caused," he grits out.

"I didn't make you sick. If you hadn't broken into my room, you wouldn't have caught what I had."

"You forgot to add fucked you senseless."

My face becomes warmer. Damn him for making me blush even over the phone.

"Whatever. The bottom line is that you need my help, and that's going to cost you."

He laughs, which turns into a coughing fit.

"God, you learn fast. Fine. Name your price."

"I want you to delete the music room video from your computer and destroy any other copies you've made."

There's another pause, which is followed by more coughing. He sounds worse than I did yesterday.

"Fine. Can you please get here quickly? And bring supplies. I got nothing."

"What kind of supplies? You have to be more specific."

"Painkillers, cold medicine, maybe some food."

I sigh loudly. "I only have painkillers and that will have to do. I'm not going shopping as I'm not feeling one-hundred-percent myself."

"Just hurry. My room is 309."

He ends the call in his usual rude style. Now that I got him to agree to delete that video, I don't feel like a doormat for helping him. I had packed the painkillers already, but I return to my room to change clothes and fix myself up a bit.

I'm preening for Jason. Someone shoot me.

I fill my bag with the few dry snacks I have and then, on a whim, I bring my violin. Maybe we can practice later if he's up to it. Before I head out, I send an email to the school's administration explaining that we're sick.

I wish I didn't bump into anyone as I head to Jason's room, but classes are about to start and there's an exodus of students making their way from the dorm to the school building. Very few people acknowledge me, that is until I stop in front of Jason's door and knock.

A couple of guys walk slower and stare as I wait for Jason to open the door. The rumor mill will be working furiously today.

"Come in," he croaks.

I open the door slowly and stick my head in first. The shades are closed, so the room is almost pitch black. I can barely make out Jason's shape on the bed. The guys in the hallway have stopped moving altogether and are now gossiping like two little bitches. I'm tempted to tell them to get lost but, in the end, I opt for not giving them more source material. I walk in and close the door fast before they can spy inside.

"Finally," Jason says. "I was beginning to think you'd changed your mind."

"Not when I'm getting something out of it."

I drop my bag and violin case on the floor, and make a beeline for the window. Then I flip the shades open to let the sunshine in.

"What the hell, Isabelle." He pulls the covers over his head.

"It was too dark. Stop bitching."

"I hate you," he mumbles.

"Yeah, we covered that already. Where's your laptop?"

His head sticks out from under the blanket so he can show me his glare. "Why do you want it?"

I watch him through narrowed eyes. "I want to see you delete the video."

With a groan, he rolls his eyes. "If I weren't in so much pain, I'd kick you out."

I spot the laptop on his nightstand, so I walk around his bed and grab it. "Here."

He yanks the device from my hand, but with him lying in bed, I can't see what he's doing. I have no choice but to get close to him.

"Move over." I nudge him with my hips as I try to find space next to him on the mattress.

"Stop being bossy."

"Stop acting like a child."

So far, my exchange with Jason today has been surreal. None of his responses have any bite. It'd be easy to mistake what we have for friendship.

He pulls up the video, but instead of deleting it, he watches it again.

"I don't need to see this. Delete it already."

"I want to watch it one more time before it's gone forever."

I start to get up, but he grabs my hand and drags it under the covers, placing it over his erection. "Help me out here, Isabelle."

"I'm not going to jerk you off!"

He gives me a puppy-dog look. His eyes are a bit glazed, and his cheeks are flushed. He must be running a fever.

"Please?" he begs.

"No." I yank my hand free. "Stop being a pest and delete the video, or I'm gone."

Pouting, he replies, "You're no fun."

I press my hand over his forehead. "Jesus, you're burning up, Jason."

"I told you I was dying."

I watch him delete the video, and I feel a little bit better but not completely. He still knows too much about me. He opens another browser, and I catch a glimpse of his email inbox. Unlike him, I don't snoop, although perhaps I should.

Instead, I bend over to grab the painkillers from my bag. For whatever reason, he thinks it's okay to snake his arm around my waist and kiss my back. Goose bumps break out on my arms as desire pools between my legs.

"What are you doing?" I ask.

He doesn't answer with words; he simply lifts my shirt and runs his tongue up my spine until he reaches my bra strap.

A shiver runs down my back, and I close my eyes. Damn it. Here he goes again, driving me insane.

"You taste so good, Isabelle. Why is that?" he whispers.

"Probably because you're not thinking straight." I twist around and shove the painkiller bottle against his chest. "Take this already before the fever damages your brain."

He takes the bottle from me, glances at it for a second, and then tosses it over his shoulder. "Later."

His hand cups my cheek, and then he kisses me. Wildfire ignites in the pit of my stomach, spreading fast over my body. His tongue tastes like toothpaste, and the mint flavor goes straight to my head. Or maybe it's him that's making my head spin.

I turn around all the way so I can kiss him properly without getting a kink in my neck. I didn't come here to make out with Jason. I honestly thought what happened yesterday was a fluke, but it seems I can't resist his dark charms.

"Why can't I stop wanting to kiss you, Isabelle?" he mumbles against my lips.

"Maybe because you don't hate me as much as you think."

"Oh, I do. I hate you with every fiber of my being. I didn't expect to want you with the same intensity."

I should stop this. Why would I want to be with someone who feels this way about me?

I push him back so I can look into his eyes. There's no trace of animosity in them. I see only desire shining there.

"I don't believe you hate me, Jason."

"Keep lying to yourself." He licks my neck, making me moan out loud.

"Tell me why then."

"No," he grumbles, and continues placing open kisses that set me on fire.

This time, I lie on my back of my own accord, but I'm surprised when he continues his caresses down my belly until he reaches the waistband of my leggings. He flicks his tongue across my skin just above the fabric and I tremble.

"I had to restrain myself yesterday. But hell, I'm tasting you now, Isabelle." He pulls my leggings and panties down just until they reach midthigh. "Look at me while I eat your pussy, beautiful."

His filthy mouth makes me even hornier. I do as he says, but I'm not prepared for the pleasure that rips me apart when he licks my clit in one long and glorious stroke.

"You like that, don't you, my dirty liar?"

"Yes," I hiss. "Maybe I should film this as payback."

He chuckles against my sex, sending another ripple of pleasure to my core. "If you wish. I don't mind, as long as you share it with me."

He returns his attention to the task, and I get lost in the sensation. I want to close my eyes, but I know he'll demand that I keep watching him. No more words are exchanged between us. Jason is determined to explore me thoroughly. I don't mind if he unveils those secrets. With an expert tongue, and fingers, he quickly brings me to the point of no return. Twisting the sheet with my hands, I throw my head back and gasp loudly.

"Scream my name, Isabelle," he says while fingering me. "Loud so everyone can hear it."

I shake my head, not wanting to give him that bit of satisfaction.

"Do it!" He inserts another finger, pressing against the G-spot Juan could never find.

No. I won't think about that monster now.

"Is that how it's going to be, then?" Jason asks. "Fine."

Suddenly, his fingers are gone. Panting like a dog and wholly unsatisfied, I look at him.

"Are you for real?" I ask.

"I asked for one simple thing, but you had to go and deny

me. Now you don't get to come." He shrugs and then licks his fingers. "Too bad. You do taste fucking delicious."

"Fine. I don't need you."

I bring my hand to my clit, knowing I'll need only a couple of flicks to climax. But Jason drags my hand away.

"Oh no. There's no do-it-yourself here, honey."

I sit up and push him back. In his debilitated state, he collapses on the mattress, and I can easily straddle him.

His eyebrows arch. "What is this? Are you going to force me? Is that it?"

I wince at his words and lose my bravado.

"No. I'd never do that." I begin to slide off him, but he stops me.

"Don't you dare." His eyes seem to burn.

I hold his stare and silently lower his boxers. I play with his length first before guiding it to my entrance. I'm so wet that he slides in effortlessly. His fingers dig into my hips as I begin to move, slowly at first. But I can't keep up this snail's pace when I was already on the verge of orgasming. I brace my palms against his chest and ride him hard.

"Say my name," he grits out, barely able to utter those words.

"Oh my God, Jason. Yes, yes, *yes!*"

"Fuck, Isabelle," he groans, pumping his hips up and down as he spills his seed inside of me.

My legs are shaking, and I can barely catch my breath. This was more cardio than I should have done while recovering from a cold. I try to get off Jason, but he keeps me in place.

"Don't go yet."

"The longer we stay in this position, the messier it will get."

"I don't care." He closes his eyes. "I like that my jizz is all over your pussy."

"I'm sure you do."

He opens one eye. "You don't mind that we haven't used protection?"

My heart constricts painfully. I drop my gaze to the hollow of his throat. "I should, but I don't."

"You're not trying to trap me with a child, are you?"

Pain flares in my chest, and this time, I do get off him.

"Hey, I was joking." He leans on his elbow.

I keep walking until I'm in his bathroom with the door closed. Even when he doesn't mean to, he manages to find my weak spots.

19

NICOLA / ISABELLE

*I*t takes me a while to recover from the post-sex conversation with Jason. That subject isn't something I let myself dwell on, like, ever. I use his shower, not caring about the significance of it when I'm stuck in my own personal hell.

I smell like him now, and that makes me feel funny—kind of giddy. Butterflies are flying freely in my belly. I shake my head. No. I'm not catching feelings for Jason. The only thing he deserves from me is animosity.

When I return to his room, he's sleeping on his stomach. One of his arms is up, hiding part of his face. He's still naked, as far as I can tell. The sheets are covering his ass. My gaze zeroes in on the painkillers on his nightstand. I assume he finally took some.

I'm developing a headache, and I feel a little woozy. I touch my forehead, finding it warm. Maybe I'm getting a fever again.

I walk around the bed and grab a couple of pills from the bottle, choosing to swallow them dry because Jason drank all the water in the glass. He sighs, and I stare at him for a moment. He looks like an angel when he's not doing horrible things and saying hateful words. My heart does a backflip.

Shit. I need to get the hell out of here. I bend over to grab my bag and violin case.

"Where are you going?" he asks in a sleepy voice.

Jesus, I thought he was knocked out.

"I already helped you in more ways than one. I'm going back to my room."

"What if I need you later?"

"I'm not your nurse, Jason. And I think I have a fever again. I just want to rest."

He flips a portion of the sheet back, confirming that he's indeed naked.

"There's plenty of space in my bed." He taps the mattress.

I'm frozen. My brain is telling me to leave, but a bigger force wants me to stay.

"Why do you want me here? You already confessed you hate me with every fiber of your being."

"Keep your enemies closer?" He smirks.

The word *no* is on the tip of my tongue, but the room begins to spin. I have to brace my hand against the nightstand and wait for the dizzy spell to pass.

"Are you going to faint?" he asks.

"I don't know."

"See? You can't leave. Who's going to take care of you?"

I stare at him, trying to guess what wicked game he's playing now. "I doubt you have good intentions in your heart."

He frowns. "I'm a good person, Isabelle."

"Your idea of good and evil is clearly different than mine."

He leans on his elbow. "I know evil. And I also know I'm not it."

That simple statement makes something click in my head. I drop my bag and case on the floor, take off my shoes, and slide next to him.

He drops his head onto the pillow while his hand rests on my hip. "That's a good girl." He smiles lazily.

"Who hurt you, Jason?"

His gaze becomes hard in an instant. He doesn't answer for a couple of beats as he holds my stare. My heart is pounding much faster now, as if it's trying to flee from my chest.

"You did," he answers finally.

I can't keep the surprise from showing on my face. I honestly expected another insult, not the naked truth. He isn't lying. Whatever he thinks I did, he believes it completely.

"How is that possible? I just met you."

He closes his eyes. "Shh. I can't think straight. Let me sleep, Isabelle. I'm tired."

Damn it. I'm tired too, but I won't be able to stop thinking about it. Even sick as a dog, Jason has the ability to torture me. It must be a talent of his.

It doesn't take long for him to start snoring softly. The noise is not that annoying, and if my brain wasn't spinning like a top, I could fall asleep easily despite the company. But now I'm obsessing about his statement. When did I hurt him? It must have happened far in the past. Maybe I met him at a violin competition. *Damn it.* I can't place him. Surely I'd remember him.

But even if I met Jason during a competition, there's no way I could have done something to him to warrant the deep-rooted hatred he feels toward me.

An idea occurs to me. I touch his cheek. "Jason?"

He doesn't react, save for turning his face the other way. I think he's truly out. It's time to do some snooping. I get out of bed slowly, careful not to wake him, and then I tiptoe toward his dresser. In the silence, everything sounds too noisy.

I don't find any clues in his drawers, so I move on to his desk. Nothing among his papers. His laptop is now lying there —he must have moved it when I was in the shower. I flip it open, and it turns on automatically. The loud *ping* as the machine starts stresses me out. I look over my shoulder, but Jason is still in dreamland.

It's a stupid risk that's probably not going to pan out. His laptop is password protected. I have nothing to lose, so I try a few combinations, which is like trying to find a needle in a haystack. I don't know enough about him to make an educated guess.

Fatigue begins to seep through my bones. I should return to bed and get some sleep. Jason mumbles my name, making me jump out of my skin. My heart is thundering as I look at him, but he isn't awake. He's mumbling my name in his sleep. Jesus, I'm in his head for real.

I try another password, my full name, and lo and behold, it works. This alone would be troubling, but when I see his screensaver picture, it feels like a punch to my stomach. It's a group picture taken after a violin competition that I won. I'm standing front and center in the image, holding my trophy. I look for Jason among the other contestants. He's all the way in the back, nearly blending in with the background with his dark hair and suit. I want to zoom in on his face, but I can't, so I squint and look closer to the screen. He's a little out of focus, but I can see it clearly now that one of his cheeks looks redder than the other. Did someone slap him before the picture was taken?

I glance at him, sleeping peacefully, and it breaks my heart. I don't know what happened, but having met his mother, I can guess. I shut the laptop and return to bed. His back is to me, so I do something insane—I wrap my arm around his waist and rest my forehead against his back.

I fall asleep spooning Jason Novak, and it's the most natural thing in the world.

***

JASON

"JASON, ARE YOU THERE?" a grating voice calls, fishing me out of a pleasant dream.

Groggy, I open my eyes, not recognizing for a second where I am. It's the warm body pressed to my back that's confusing me. Then I remember. I asked Isabelle to stay, and she's now glued to me in a spooning position. I go through a gamut of emotions in the span of a few seconds. I'm torn between shoving her off me and basking in the proximity. My body decides for me and melts into her. I'd be able to enjoy the moment if the banging on my door would cease.

"Jason, don't make me call maintenance to open this door," Sloane continues.

Isabelle drops her arm from my waist and rolls away from me. There goes my chance of teasing her for it.

"Who's that?" she croaks. "And what time is it?"

I get up, not bothering to answer her questions. I'm in a foul mood, but I don't want to take it out on her. I must be feverish still. Naked, I stride to the door and yank it open.

"What?"

Sloane's eyes widen, but at least she doesn't drop her gaze to my crotch.

"You missed class, and you didn't answer your phone. I was worried."

"I got a cold."

"You do look awful." She raises her hand to touch my forehead, but I lean back.

"Yeah, you woke me up. If all you wanted was proof of life, you have it."

Her gaze travels past my shoulder, and it's like a switch is flipped. From concerned to angry in zero point two seconds.

"What is *she* doing here?" she shrieks.

I cross my arms and smirk. "She couldn't stay away, and I'm not one to deny myself pussy even if I'm dying."

Sloane's expression twists into a scowl. "You're fucking that bitch? I thought you hated her."

I expect Isabelle to jump into the conversation, and when she doesn't, I look over my shoulder. She's sleeping. A bubble of laughter goes up my throat. Either she's super sick, or she's so unfazed by Sloane's presence that she can't be bothered to join us.

"I don't owe you any explanation. Goodbye, Sloane." I shut the door in her face and return to bed, smiling from ear to ear.

"That was cold, Jason. I thought she was your friend," Isabelle says without opening her eyes.

I slide next to her and pull her closer. "Were you pretending to be asleep?"

"Not pretending, trying to get back to sleep. But she was too loud."

"I'm surprised there wasn't a catfight."

She opens her eyes. "You would love that, wouldn't you?"

My smile broadens. "It does have its appeal."

"Guys are stupid." She begins to shut her eyes again.

"Yes."

I'm still smiling like a goof, and I don't know why. What the hell is happening here? I fucked this girl twice, and now I'm enjoying being nice to her? Maybe I'm too sick to think of something hateful to say or do. That must be it. I haven't forgotten all the years of humiliation and psychological abuse I went through because of her.

If only she'd been nice to me so many years ago, maybe I wouldn't have channeled all my energy into hating her.

I touch her forehead. "I think your fever is gone. You can go back to your room now."

"Are you kicking me out?"

I want to say *No, I want you to stay*, but I can't trust myself in this weakened state. I've already been too soft around her.

"Yes. You've served your purpose."

"You'll have to physically drag me out of here, then. I'm not moving on my own."

"Are you daring me, Isabelle?"

She watches me through slitted eyes. "I know you don't have any reservations about doing it, but I doubt that you can actually carry me right now."

I narrow my gaze. "I'm not that sick. I felt worse earlier and I still had enough stamina to fuck you, didn't I?"

"Correction, I fucked you. You just lay there like a corpse."

She's pushing my buttons on purpose. I don't know what the hell she's trying to accomplish here. She knows I can wreak havoc on her life.

"Do you want me to hurt you, Isabelle? Is that your kink?"

"If you're asking me if I like chains and whips, no, Jason, I don't."

I glance at her neck, remembering choking her a bit as I fucked her. I get a hard-on almost instantly. Jesus, and I feel like I've been run over by a truck. I can't imagine what it'll be like fucking her when I'm not dying.

I run my fingers over her neck, then flatten my palm there. "But you like it rough, don't you?"

She doesn't answer right away, but her eyes never waver from mine. "Only with you," she says.

Her words feel like a punch to my chest, and for a moment, I can't breathe right. I'm still struggling to find words when she continues, "You were in Switzerland for a violin competition when you were ten."

My eyes widen of their own accord, and my pulse accelerates. "You remember me?"

She shakes her head. "I don't remember much about that day, to be honest. I don't even remember playing. On the way to the venue, we received the news that my grandmother had passed away. I was close to her. I didn't want to compete, but my parents insisted. The prize was too important."

And don't I know it.

She closes her eyes for a second. "They convinced me that was what my grandma would have wanted."

A tear rolls from her eye, and I wipe it off with my thumb.

Why am I allowing her sappy story to move me this way? People die all the time.

"What did I do to you that day, Jason?" She pleads for an answer with her bright eyes.

I clench my jaw hard and then look away. "It doesn't matter. Nothing you can say now will change how I feel about you."

I sense her move, but I refuse to look when she gets up. I can still see her movements from the corner of my eye. She grabs her bag and violin case and slips out of my room without another word.

20

NICOLA / ISABELLE

I don't like how I allowed Jason to nudge his way into my heart. Despite all the horrible things he's done to me so far, my head is filled with guilt because of him. My chest aches as if it's been bruised—or is trying to recover from heartache. I wish I could talk to someone about him, but the closest person to a friend I have here isn't talking to me.

I head to school early, trying to avoid bumping into Jason on the way. I have no idea if he's coming today, but I also stopped myself from checking on him. I must remember we aren't friends; we're enemies who allowed the lines to blur and had hate sex.

I text Sage again, hoping she'll reply. I wish I had talked to her more. If I knew her schedule, I could wait in front of her class. But destiny will have it that I bump into Justice in the

He's alone, and when he sees me making a beeline for him, he tenses.

"Hey, Nicola. I've been meaning to thank you for paying for lunch the other day."

Thank me? You should be coughing up the money, you ass. I have a bigger issue to bring up though. "Whatever. What did you say to Sage?"

His expression changes from friendly to wary in the blink of an eye. "What makes you think I talked to her at all?"

"You went after her on Saturday. Don't insult my intelligence by claiming you didn't catch up with her."

He looks around in a cagey manner. He's probably making sure we don't have an audience. It's early, so no one is at school yet.

"Listen, I like Sage, okay? I'm sorry you got the wrong idea about us."

My eyebrows shoot to the heavens. "The only idea I got is that you have no sense of boundaries. If Sage arrived at the wrong conclusion, that's your fault, not mine."

He runs a hand through his hair. "True. I didn't say anything about you. I swear."

I watch him through narrowed eyes. He sounds sincere, but there's something off about him. My sixth sense is telling me he's a snake.

"I hope you didn't. I'd hate it if Luke found out about Saturday."

A gleam of annoyance shines in his eyes. "Are you blackmailing me, Nicola?"

I shrug. "This isn't blackmail. Just a warning that if you lied to Sage about what happened at the diner, there will be consequences."

He steps into my personal space, leaning down for a menacing effect. "I'm not afraid of you, bitch. Say a word, and you'll be the sorry one."

A bubble of laughter goes up my throat. "Are you seriously threatening me, Justice?"

"Yeah, Justice. Are you?" Jason asks from behind me.

Shit. I so didn't want him to witness my exchange with this douche canoe.

Justice steps back from me at once, looking positively ill. "This isn't what it looks like."

Jason steps forward and stands next to me. His hand finds my lower back in a possessive way, and Justice doesn't miss the gesture. "Is that so? What did I just witness, then? Explain it to me."

"I…" His gaze darts to mine as if he wants my help coming up with an excuse.

"You what?" Jason snaps. "Can't come up with a half-baked excuse on the fly? Maybe I should tell Luke you're still sniffing around his sister and let him deal with you."

Justice's tanned face goes a shade paler. Why does everyone here seem to be afraid of what Luke can do? Is he some kind of a menace?

He glares at me. "Did you tell him about Saturday?"

I don't care for his accusatory tone one bit.

"I'd listen to Jason if I were you. Leave Sage alone," I reply.

He shakes his head. "Unbelievable. It doesn't matter if you're the king or the weirdo, you rich kids are all the same."

Jason snaps. He grabs Justice by his collar and shoves him against the locker. "Do not disrespect Nicola, motherfucker."

"Let go of me."

Jason pulls him forward only to push him against the locker again harder. "I've been lenient with you, but if I find out you're still bothering Nicola or Sage, I'll make sure you never set foot in this school again. Is that clear?"

He steps back and releases Justice, who seems about to piss in his pants.

"Get out of my sight. Your pathetic face is making me sick."

Without a word, Justice scrambles away and disappears around the corner.

"You're welcome," Jason says without looking at me.

"I didn't ask for your assistance."

He turns around and walks over to me. I don't dare breathe, waiting for his next move. He's still riding the anger from dealing with Justice, and he's about to unleash what's left on me. Oddly, I'm not afraid.

He grabs my face roughly, igniting the damn butterflies in my stomach.

"When is it going to dawn on you, Isabelle? Only *I* can hurt you."

I bat his hand away and step back. "You can try."

Pissed that I can't control how my body reacts to my tormentor, I walk around him without a thought to where I'm going.

I should have known Jason wouldn't let me have the last word, he never does. He catches up with me, looping his arm around my waist to steer me through the open door to my right. It's one of the few classrooms that doesn't have huge windows facing the hallway.

"What the hell!"

He spins me around, pushing me against the wall. "I'm not going to try, Isabelle. I *will* succeed."

My retort is cut by his mouth claiming mine. There's nothing sweet about this kiss. It's feral and possessive, and I love it. Damn, it's crazy how much I do. His entire body is pressed against mine, and his hands are already under my skirt. I don't want him to have all the fun. Since I can't hide how much I want him, I might as well go for it.

I reach for his zipper, but my hands are clumsy, and I fumble with it. Or maybe I'm too distracted by Jason's fingers slipping inside my pussy.

"I love how wet you get for me, Isabelle."

A moan escapes my lips. I throw my head back, closing my eyes and forgetting Jason's cock for a moment.

"Are you enjoying yourself, darling?" he whispers near my lips.

"Yes."

He pulls his fingers out just as it's beginning to feel really good. I'm still dazed, so I don't fight when Jason steers me toward the desk. He turns me around and pushes me roughly over it, keeping his hand behind my head so my cheek is flattened against the hard surface.

The sound of fabric being torn is the only warning I get before he plunges into me. With me bent over like this, he can go much deeper and he's not playing nice. It hurts, but it also feels amazing.

"Are you still enjoying yourself?" he asks between grunts.

I tighten my walls around him in response, and he curses.

"God, why does your pussy feel so good, Isabelle?"

Whether he's being rhetorical or not, I wouldn't be able to answer him. The room is spinning, and my body is quickly disintegrating under him. I try not to moan when I climax, but my shudders are telltale. Jason groans loudly, pumping his seed into me. He keeps fucking me even when cum drips down my legs. With a final hard push, he leans forward and draws his tongue across my cheek.

"Did you come, my filthy little liar?"

"You know the answer to that."

"Did it hurt?" He bites my earlobe.

"No."

"Don't tease me, sweetheart. You know how hard I get when you lie."

He pulls out, allowing me to stand straighter. When I turn, his pants are zipped up, and he's watching me with a smug smile.

"Did you get your fill?" I ask.

"This will do for the next couple of hours." He bends over and picks up scraps of black fabric—what's left of my underwear.

"Don't bother wearing these to school. They'll get ripped off every damn time." He pockets my panties and heads to the door.

The brutal reality finally drops like a bomb. Jason fucked me at school where anyone could have seen us, and I let him. Worse, I enjoyed the danger of potential discovery. Now I have to take care of the messy situation underneath my skirt.

Jason stops by the door and looks over his shoulder. "Are you coming?"

"I have to deal with the evidence first."

His eyes darken. "If you're thinking about cleaning up, forget it."

"Excuse me?"

"You're going to class today with my jizz all over you, darling." He smiles like the devil he is.

My jaw drops. "Why?"

"Because it makes me happy." He waves me over. "Come on. We don't wanna be late for English."

"I don't have English in the first period."

"You do now."

"You changed my *schedule*?" My voice rises to a shriek.

His grin broadens. "I can't torture you to my heart's content if I don't see you all the time, can I?"

21

JASON

*T*he moment I saw that punk getting up close and personal with Isabelle, it took incredible restraint on my part not to break his face. But with my mother in town, I can't beat the shit out of the basketball team star without getting in trouble with the headmaster, and in consequence, her.

She's staying until the damn recital is over, which means flying under her radar is crucial if I'm to survive the rest of the month without imploding.

I'm glad that I have Isabelle to distract me.

She was quiet during English, probably uncomfortable with her post-O-town look. We both smelled like sex, and I made sure she sat right next to me. It wouldn't take much to conclude she was my morning delight.

The moment the bell rings, she jumps from her seat and rushes to the door.

I smile. *Go on, my little lamb, run away from me. The best part of the hunt is the chase.*

"What's with the happy face?" Corbin Monteiro, a supersmart dude who's usually not a pain in the ass, asks.

I shake my head. "Nada."

"Uh-huh. Nothing. I can guess who put that goofy grin on your sour face."

"What? Can't I be in a good mood without a reason?" I ask innocently.

"You're a Novak, so the answer is no."

I sigh in my head. Corbin isn't wrong. My family founded this town, so everything that happens in our circle eventually becomes gossip, and the stories are never fairy tales. They're fucked up and mostly true. Happiness is a word that doesn't exist in the Novak vocabulary.

"You got close to the new girl fast," Corbin continues. "I thought that once you decided to get serious, it would be with Sloane."

I don't like the way this conversation is going. Glowering, I ask, "Where did you get the notion that I'm with Nicola?"

His eyebrows rise, almost meeting his hairline. "Oh shit, you aren't?"

"No," I growl.

He lifts both hands, palms facing me. "Sorry. Don't need to go savage on my ass. I just got a vibe from you two."

"There's no vibe," I grit out. "So you'd better keep your piehole shut about this."

I hoist my backpack over my shoulder and stride out of the room before I indeed go savage on his ass. It takes me a minute to calm down. I used to be able to control my emotions better. It doesn't take much to get a rise in my temper lately. It's all because of Isabelle. She's messing with my head big-time, and I can't stop it.

We're supposed to practice at the end of the day, but if I

don't get into a better state of mind, I'll end up hate fucking her again, and there goes violin rehearsal. As much as I want to punish her, I don't want to blow the performance. I know I don't need my mother's approval, but the desire to please her is ingrained in my soul. Old habits are hard to break, and she's a master of psychological warfare.

Unlike most fucks who stumble through life not knowing why they act in destructive ways, I'm very much aware of my issues. I just can't do anything about them.

I'm lost in thought, so I don't notice Finn until he steps up next to me.

"Have you heard the awesome news?" he asks me.

"By your sarcastic tone, it isn't great, and it involves our family," I grumble.

"We're having a party. Well, your mother is having a party, but that means all Novaks must be in attendance. Even my sister is coming."

I stop walking to stare at him. "You're joking."

"I wish I was. I was hoping we could go back to Playground this weekend."

My head hurts just thinking about another Novak social event. They're torture, and if my mother is the hostess, that means I'll have to play for her guests. She enjoys putting me on display only to tear me apart later.

I fish out my phone and check for messages from her. She didn't call, but I do find an email she sent an hour ago.

"Are you bringing Nicola to the party?" Finn asks.

The look I give him is answer enough. "Why would I do that?"

He shrugs. "No reason. I just know it will be a huge party, and the invitation extends to older offspring too. I had to listen to Tara bitch about it on the phone this morning. She so doesn't want to fly in from New Haven for this."

"Great," I groan. "That means half of Maverick Prep will be there."

"It's unlike your mother to throw anything last minute. Do you have any idea why she's doing it?"

I grind my teeth. "Maybe."

"You're not going to tell me, are you?"

"No. It's not that I don't trust you, but you have enough on your plate dealing with your asshole father."

"I don't mind. Misery loves company. But it's fine, man. I get it."

"Are any of you fools bringing a date?" I ask so I can change the subject.

He laughs. "Hell to the fucking no. Anyway, I gotta run or I'll be late, and Mr. Kaufman will have my balls."

I watch him sprint down the hallway and then I veer in the opposite direction. I need a break from school, from all these people wanting to know about my personal life. I'll come back for practice with Isabelle.

Most of the time, I don't let the scrutiny bother me, and there are perks that come with being the king of this fucking school. Today, I feel the full weight of being a Novak, and it's too much.

22

NICOLA / ISABELLE

I ignore Jason's order and make a beeline to the restroom. I'm not going to parade around school smelling like a sex dungeon. He doesn't follow me, but that means nothing. I want to know how he was able to change my schedule without my consent. I don't even know if I'm still enrolled in my next class.

The bell rings, telling me I either have to go to advanced math or skip it in order to complain to the school administration. I don't want to be told by the teacher that I'm no longer in his class if Jason changed that too.

The lady behind the office desk lifts her gaze from her computer and immediately twists her face into a scowl. "What are you doing here, Ms. Devlin? Don't you have class?"

"I don't know, to be honest. My schedule was changed without my knowledge."

She widens her eyes, only to narrow them in the next second. "That isn't possible. Any changes to a student's schedule at this point must be approved by the headmaster."

Either Jason lied to me about changing my schedule and the English teacher was too scared of him to say anything, or he has more power in this school than I thought.

"Could you please check my schedule? I want to make sure I'm still enrolled in all the classes I selected."

Her lips become a thin flat line, but she does print out a copy for me.

"Here." She slides the piece of paper across the counter.

Son of a bitch. Jason lied. I was supposed to have gone to history, not English. That fucking asshole. I curl my hands around the paper, wrinkling it.

"Was your schedule changed?" she asks.

"No. It seems I was the victim of a prank."

"You'll have to file a complaint, or you'll receive an unexcused absence for the class you missed."

I don't see a point in telling her about Jason. Nothing will happen to him.

"I'll think about it."

Judging by her frown, she doesn't like my answer.

"You'd better get to your next class. Better to receive a tardy than not go altogether."

"Right. Thanks."

I plan on doing just that, but then I see Sage head into the library. She must have study hall. Screw math, I'd rather clear the air with her instead. I hurry down the hallway, trying to avoid being spotted by a faculty member.

Sage is sitting alone at a desk by the window and doesn't notice me until I pull up a chair next to her.

"Hi," I whisper.

Her brows furrow. "What are you doing here?"

There's no point beating around the bush, so I cut straight to the chase. "I saw you come in. You've been avoiding my texts and calls. Are you mad at me because of Justice?"

She clenches her jaw and then glances down. "Yes."

"I don't like Justice, like not even a little bit."

She glances at me again. "Then why did you guilt him into having lunch with you?"

"*Guilt* him? Is that what he told you?"

"He said he saved you from being run over by a car and that you insisted on paying for his lunch. He felt bad saying no, but he wasn't keen."

That rotten piece of shit.

I count to ten in my head before I reply. If I bad-mouth the asshole, most likely Sage will take his side. Infatuation turns people blind.

"That's not what happened. We were both heading to Dennis's Diner and figured we could keep each other company. I don't know why he would twist the truth."

A shadow of doubt crosses her eyes. At least she's not refuting my idea completely.

She shakes her head and looks out the window. "I don't know what to think anymore. I really, really like him. But Luke hates his guts and... well, I know Justice can get any girl he wants."

Jesus. It sounds like Sage is head over heels in love with the guy. I don't know what to say to open her eyes. She'd have to see him doing something shady to believe he's bad news.

"He can't get me. He's not my type."

She turns to me again, tilting her head. "You like Jason, don't you?"

Blush spreads through my cheeks. "I don't like him. He's an ass."

Her lips twist into a smile. "I was stupid for getting jealous of you with Justice. You're totally into Jason. I can see it now."

"You're imagining things." I stand. "What are you doing on Saturday?"

"I'm not sure. I think I need to go buy a gown for Victoria Petrov's party."

The mention of Jason's mother turns my blood cold. "She's having a party? When?"

"On Saturday. It's super last minute, but when you're filthy rich, you can make things happen in a short period of time."

Jason didn't say anything about a party, but why would he? We're not a couple.

"I can help you shop for a dress," I say.

"That would be fun," she replies with a smile, but it wilts quickly. "Oh, crap. Were you not invited?"

"Nope. But that's fine. I've met Victoria, and I'm not looking for a repeat."

Despite my answer, guilt shines in Sage's eyes.

"Don't look at me like that. I really don't care that I wasn't invited. Truly."

"Okay."

"I'll text you later."

I walk out of the library, hoping that Sage bought my lie. I shouldn't be upset about the stupid party, but the sadness swirling in my chest says otherwise.

I have at least twenty minutes to kill before my next class, so I decide to grab something to eat at the cafeteria. I'm halfway there when my name is called through the speakers.

"Ms. Nicola Devlin, please report to the headmaster's office at once."

Crap on toast. What the hell did I do now? Am I in trouble with Mr. Cain because I ditched a couple of classes? If that's the case, is calling me through the speakers necessary?

I'm annoyed as hell as I march to his office. His assistant looks at me and widens her eyes when she picks up on my mood.

"Mr. Cain wanted to see me?"

"Yes, you can go in. He's waiting for you."

I don't knock, and I make sure I shut the door hard so he knows I'm angry.

"What did I do now?" I ask, ignoring the chair.

He looks at me with a troubled gaze, and I don't think it has anything to do with my attitude.

"Why don't you sit down, Nicola?"

"I'm fine standing."

"Very well. Your parents called me with disturbing news."

All my anger whooshes out of my chest like a party balloon, and a heaviness sets there. I haven't talked to them in weeks.

"You spoke to them? When?"

"Half an hour ago."

"Why? What happened?"

I'm shaking now from head to toe. Maybe I should have listened to Mr. Cain and sat down. But my knees are locked tight, and the best I can do is brace my hands on the back of the chair.

"Your grave was desecrated last night."

I turn into a statue made of ice. I can't breathe, I can't blink. My pulse is beating loudly in my ears as I process the news.

"Do they know who did it?" I force the question out.

Of course they know. The only person who would want to open my coffin is Juan. Now he knows I'm not dead.

"No. The police have nothing, but...."

"There's only one person with a motive."

I run my fingers through my hair, pulling my bangs back in the process. Mr. Cain's eyes lock on my scar, but I don't care.

"H-how did they find out about my grave?" I ask.

"The cemetery administration called the police, and then it made the local news."

And my parents' lawyer in Barcelona must have called them. He's the only one in Spain who knows where they live now.

"Is my parents' location still safe?"

He nods. "I believe so. No one knows they're in Costa Rica."

Relief eases the constriction in my chest, but not by much.

"What does that mean for me? Do I need to move again?"

Pity shines in his eyes, and I hate it. "It means that you have to be extra careful. They won't be able to contact you for a while. They already took a risk reaching out to me."

I press a fist against my chest, trying to ease the ache. The panic hasn't set in completely yet, but it will flare up later, I'm sure. "I... I think I need to lie down."

"You may take the rest of the day off. You won't get in trouble for missing any classes, including the first and second periods you ditched."

"Thank you."

I walk out of his office in a daze, seeing nothing.

23

JASON

*B*lowing off all my classes does little to make me less edgy, but as I drive back to school, another feeling becomes stronger. I can't determine what it is, only that I'm anxious to see Isabelle and play the violin with her.

I was obsessed with the girl before I knew her, but now she's become a veritable drug to me.

My eyes immediately search for her as I enter the music room. Everyone is there, including Sloane, who doesn't hide the glower.

"Oh, Jason, there you are," Mrs. Simpson greets me.

"Where's Nicola?"

"She's not coming today."

Annoyance erupts from the pit of my stomach. She'd better not be blowing me off on purpose. "Why not?"

"I'm not sure. I only received an email from Mr. Cain telling me she was excused from classes today."

My hands curl into fists. "That's bullshit."

Mrs. Simpson's expression twists into a scowl. "Excuse me?"

"She shouldn't get a free pass."

"Maybe she's sick," Sloane pipes up with a sly grin on her face.

My gaze narrows, but I don't have time to deal with her right now. I turn around and head for the door.

"Jason, where do you think you're going?" Mrs. Simpson asks.

"If Nicola isn't here, there's no reason for me to stay."

She retorts, but I don't pay attention to the words. I'm too lost in my fury to give a shit about teachers and school. I head back to the dorms, ready to give Isabelle the punishment she deserves.

I don't knock on her door, I use my master key instead only to discover the door wasn't locked in the first place.

"You'd better be dying or there'll be hell to pay," I say as I stride into her room.

She's sitting on her bed, facing the window, and doesn't move a muscle in reaction to my big entrance. I kick the door closed hard and reach her in a few long strides.

"What are you do—" I stop midsentence when I see the dead glint in her eyes. I grab her shoulders, leaning forward. "Isabelle?"

She doesn't answer, she doesn't even blink. It's like she's blind to the world around her.

I shake her a little. "Isabelle, talk to me."

The little jolt seems to awaken her from the daze. She blinks a couple of times as her eyes set on my face. "It's over," she mumbles.

My gut twists painfully. I have no idea what she's talking about, but it sounds absolute, unchangeable. "What's over?"

"My life."

"Your life isn't over," I grit out.

"He knows I'm not dead."

My stomach sinks, and everything begins to make sense. The asshole who hurt Isabelle, who tried to take her away from me, is on her trail. My heart is beating at a staccato, fighting all the emotions swirling inside. The hate I cultivated all these years crumbles like a sandcastle. I can't hold on to it when there's a real chance I might lose Isabelle forever. The agony I felt when I believed she'd died is not something I want to go through again.

I capture her face between my hands. "He's not going to find you."

"You don't know him. He's resourceful."

"So am I. He'll have to go through me to get to you, darling."

She closes her eyes as her expression crumples. "I don't need a fake knight in shining armor, Jason. Don't pretend you're my savior just because a bigger bully is threatening to take away your toy."

"You're not a toy, damn it!"

She looks into my eyes. "Prove it."

How do I prove something that hasn't even taken proper shape in my head? My feelings for her are blurry and turbulent. When I don't answer immediately, she begins to lean away from me.

Fuck it. That's it. It's time to step off the edge. The fall might destroy me or set me free.

I kiss her, but it's not the bruising, rough kisses she's used to receiving from me. It's tender, and so damn sweet, it might give me a toothache. Her lips are soft and pliable, but her tongue is fire. With a groan, I deepen the kiss, tilting her head to the side so I can drown in her. My pulse is going a hundred miles an hour, and the sense that I'm free-falling is real.

Euphoria is making my heart beat at the speed of light. I refuse to look too closely at the reasons. I nudge her back until we're both lying in bed, facing each other. I'm burning for her, but today, I want to take things slowly, so I run my fingers down her arms, wishing they were bare. She took off her uniform jacket at one point, but the button-down shirt is still in place.

Her arm sneaks around my waist, and then she grabs the back of my jacket, twisting the fabric with her fingers. We don't speak, we don't break apart for air. I don't know what's on her mind, but all I can think about is how right it feels to be with her.

I surrender to the emotions as I explore her body with my hands. Crazy giddiness makes me laugh when I discover she's still naked underneath her skirt. I take my time playing with her, alternating between teasing her clit with my fingers and fucking her with them. Her moans and sighs breathe life into me.

"Jason... I need you."

"I'm right here, babe." I kiss the corner of her mouth.

"I want you inside of me."

Ah hell. There goes my idea of making out for hours. I can't deny her request when it makes my balls so tight, I'm afraid I'll lose my mind if I don't fuck her right this second.

I jump off the bed to get rid of my clothes. Isabelle leans on her elbows and watches me with heat in her eyes. Her lips are red and a little swollen already, making them even more kissable.

I'm dying to get back in bed with her, but I don't hurry. I shrug off my jacket first, and then unbutton my shirt painfully slowly. Her chest is heaving, making her breasts strain against the fabric that covers them.

When her eyes drop to my naked chest, it brings a satisfied smile to my lips. "Do you like what you see, darling?"

She flicks her gaze back to mine. "You know I do. You've always been the handsome devil I couldn't resist."

I couldn't resist you either, beautiful.

The thought remains unspoken. It's too open, too honest.

"It's your turn now."

Her hands are shaking as she unfastens her shirt's buttons.

"Are you nervous?" I ask.

She nods as she parts her top. Her bra is simple cotton and a little see-through. But it fastens in the front. With a flick of her fingers, she releases the clasp. It just occurred to me that I've never taken the time to appreciate her breasts properly. And now I can't wait to feast on them.

"Your pants." Her voice is raspy and sultry.

Jesus, this girl will be my undoing.

Who are you kidding, Jason? She already is.

I get rid of my pants and briefs in one movement, but I'm done staying away from her. I pounce, aiming first for her sweet pussy. She opens her legs for me as I disappear underneath her skirt. I love her taste so damn much. I flick my tongue across her clit and then suck the little nub into my mouth. She arches her back, letting out a throaty moan that almost makes me come on the spot.

"Oh my God, Jason. You're..."

"I'm what, darling?"

She yells a string of words as her body shatters underneath my tongue. *Man, that must have been a record.* I keep eating her pussy, despite her protests that she can't take it anymore. It's only when she curls her fingers around strands of my hair and yanks hard that I stop.

"Jason!"

"What?" I ask innocently.

"I'm already in pieces," she laughs.

I kiss her inner thigh before I make the trip back to her face. Her tits are begging for my attention, but I need to be inside her first.

"Be prepared to be pulverized then." I kiss her tenderly as I slide home.

Home. I hide my face in the crook of her neck and don't move as I process the thought.

"Jason?"

"Yes?"

"Are you okay?"

I lean back to look into her eyes. "More than okay."

Focusing on her lovely face, I resume what I started, knowing very well the difference between what's happening now and all the other times we fucked. I stop the words from forming in my head, focusing on what's happening down below. It's not hard when she feels so fucking amazing.

Her name is on my tongue when I climax, and something else too. But I don't say it. I will never say it. This secret I'll take to the grave.

24

NICOLA / ISABELLE

I fall asleep in Jason's arms. When I wake up, we're still twisted in a lover's embrace. It's dark outside, but I have no idea how many hours have passed since Jason came into my room. I lift my head, craning my neck to check my phone for the time.

Jason groans, tightening his hold on me. "Don't go," he says, half asleep.

"I just want to check the time."

He kisses my shoulder and squeezes my ass. "I'll tell you what time it is."

Tingles of desire trickle down my back, but I can't keep using sex to forget what happened earlier. Fear is already crawling its way into my chest, squeezing my heart like a boa constrictor.

"What's the matter?" he asks through a frown.

"I'm afraid, Jason."

He caresses my cheek with the tips of his fingers. "Don't be. I won't let anything happen to you."

"You hate me. Why do you care about my safety?"

"I…" He stops as if he doesn't know what to say. Then he drops his gaze to my lips and runs his thumb over them. "You were right. I don't hate you."

Warmth spreads through my chest, competing with the darkness there.

"What did Juan do to you?" he asks, looking into my eyes again.

The question is triggering. I don't want to relive my worst nightmare, but something in Jason's eyes makes me want to spill all my secrets.

"We dated for two years. I was a freshman, and he was a sophomore."

Jason's face twists into something akin to deep agony. Is it because I dated another guy?

"He was the perfect boyfriend until he became jealous and possessive. He hated how much time I spent practicing the violin. At the end of my sophomore year, I found out he had cheated on me, so I ended things."

I take a deep breath, closing my eyes for a second. "Then he tricked me into going to his family's vacation home in a secluded area in Spain. I thought it was a group trip."

Tears gather in my eyes as the memories flood my brain.

"It's okay, Isabelle. You're safe now. He's not going to hurt you."

I let out a shuddering exhale before I continue. "He made me his prisoner. I was locked in a boarded-up room for days. My parents didn't know what was happening. He kept my phone and sent text messages to them pretending to be me. He forced me to send video updates."

Jason's eyes spark with fury, and his jaw locks tight.

"All the while he kept saying I was never going to leave him again, and he described in detail all the horrible things he'd do to me and my parents if I tried to escape."

I swallow hard, afraid of how Jason is going to react when I tell him the most depraved part of my ordeal.

"I was terrified of him, but at that point, he hadn't petrified me into hopelessness yet. The next time he forced me to shoot a video for my parents, I tried to signal to them that I was in trouble. He figured it out."

Jason reaches for my arm, and the contact works as an anchor to ground me in the present, in the safety of my room and his company.

"The following night, he didn't come to visit me. He brought a girl, or a woman, I don't know her age. All I remember are her screams, begging for him to stop whatever he was doing. He tortured someone for *hours*, knowing I could hear her, to show what would happen to me."

I'm shocked when Jason's eyes well up with tears. I didn't think he'd ever cry, at least not about something that happened to me.

"He did that for three nights in a row. Three girls suffered because of me. I know that because he used their names. He wanted me to know he had brought a new victim." I shut my eyes. "I can still hear their screams."

"It wasn't your fault, sweetheart," he says.

"If it weren't for me, they'd still be alive."

He doesn't argue with me, and I'm glad about that. My parents and therapists gave me the same spiel. But they weren't there. They didn't live through the nightmare.

"How did you escape?"

"I knew that Juan would keep hurting more girls because of me, so I decided that the only way to stop him was to escape or die trying. When he finally came to visit me, still wearing blood-stained clothes, I seduced him."

Jason's gaze becomes darker as he narrows his eyes.

"I didn't sleep with him. I led him on, and when he was distracted, I used the lamp to knock him unconscious. Then I ran and didn't stop."

"You said he killed you."

"He caught up with me and beat me to within an inch of my life. I passed out, and when I woke up, I was in a hospital. My parents told me a truck driver found me by the road."

Jason wipes off the moisture from my cheeks. I didn't notice I had been crying. Then he pulls me into his arms and hugs me tight.

"If that motherfucker ever steps foot in Triton Cove, he's done."

Being protected by Jason should make me feel better, but instead, it makes me more worried. Despite our turbulent and messed-up relationship, I care about him, which means he's the first person that Juan will try to hurt to get to me.

"Please don't get in the way, Jason. If Juan finds me, then it's over."

He pushes me back and glares. "How can you expect me to not do anything and just let him take you away from me again?"

"Again? When was I ever yours?"

He pulls me against his chest again and kisses my forehead. "You're mine, Isabelle, and no one messes with what belongs to a Novak. No one."

I tense in his arms. "Juan also thought I was his. I'll never allow anyone to put me in a cage again, Jason."

"I don't want to put you in a cage."

"What do you want from me, then?"

He doesn't answer for a couple of beats. "I want you to stay."

Something in his tone makes my heart skip a beat. I don't say it out loud, but I want to stay too, and not only because I'm tired of running. I want to stay because of him.

NICOLA / ISABELLE

*A*n elbow against my ribs wakes me from sleep and I yelp, rolling away from the intruder and ending up on the floor. My heart is about to burst out of my chest as adrenaline kicks in.

Jason's sleepy face appears above me. "Are you okay?"

My heart is thumping too fast, and it hurts. I press a hand between my breasts as I try to catch my breath. "You scared me."

The corners of his lips twitch upward. "You fell off the bed because of me?"

I get back to my feet, realizing I'm naked when his gaze drops to my boobs. I cover them with my arms. "I wasn't expecting anyone in my bed."

"You forgot that I spent the night? I'm wounded." He smiles.

Resting my head in my hand, I breathe out. "There's been a lot to process. But why did you stay?"

He turns serious then, furrowing his brows. "Because I

wanted to. Are you going to question every decision I make in relation to you now?"

"No. Only the ones that are sus."

His eyebrows shoot to the heavens. "How is me spending the night suspicious?"

When I don't reply, he wraps an arm around my waist and pulls me close, then kisses my belly. "What guy in their right mind would pass up the chance to wake up next to you?"

I push him back and step away from his embrace. "Yeah, I forgot for a moment that guys have one-track minds."

He smirks. "Speaking of which…" He pauses and points at his erection. "Any chance you wanna take care of this?"

The fact he's asking and not demanding that I blow him is enough to make my head spin. I watch him closely. "What are you plotting now, Jason?"

He stands in a huff. "Jeez, if you're not in the mood for a quickie, you just have to say so."

My jaw drops to the floor as I watch him veer for my bathroom and close the door. Who is this guy, and what has he done with Jason? Maybe his system is still overloaded with all the baggage I dumped on him last night.

I can't believe I was able to tell the whole story without crumbling to bits. I was close to having a nervous breakdown, but he helped me through it all. It's insane that my bully would be the one person I'd be able to tell about my darkest hour without losing my shit.

The toilet flushes, and a second later, Jason walks out.

"You're still naked. Does that mean you've changed your mind about sexy times?"

Sex with Jason is always a good idea, but once I glance at the time, I know we've run out of it. "We have ten minutes to get ready. I don't want to be late."

An emotion flashes in his eyes. "Does that mean you're staying?"

I never said I'd leave Triton Cove, but I suppose after learning about Juan, Jason concluding that I'd pack and go isn't illogical.

"I'm done running away from that monster."

A dangerous glint shines in his eyes as he walks over. "Good. But if he finds you, I want you to be ready."

"Ready for what?"

"To end him."

When I think Jason can't surprise me anymore, he proves me wrong.

"What happened to all that talk of being my protector?" I tease, because I can't deal with his statement at face value right now.

Holding my stare, he cups my cheek. "Oh, if that scum crosses my path first, make no mistake, I'll be the last person he sees. But I have to consider the possibility he'll find you first."

My stomach twists into savage knots, making me queasy. I don't want to talk about that possibility. Yes, I'm sticking my head in the sand, but it hasn't been twenty-four hours since I learned Juan violated my tomb. I haven't processed the news properly yet.

"We need to get ready for school," I say.

Jason squints, knowing I'm blowing him off. "Fine. But this conversation isn't over."

He collects his clothes, which are scattered on the floor, and gets dressed. I just stand there and watch because, despite all my problems, I'm not blind, and the boy is damn fine.

Before he leaves, he kisses me softly on the lips. "I'll be back in five."

I don't move from my spot for a minute after he walks out the door. Jason being sweet is too surreal for me to accept as reality. I can't let my guard down around him.

By a miracle, I'm ready when Jason returns exactly five minutes later. He doesn't use his key; instead he knocks and waits outside. When the donation is too much, the saint mistrusts. No one can blame me for being leery of his intentions.

He changed clothes and his hair is damp. Also, his five o'clock shadow is gone.

"I can't believe you had time to shower *and* shave."

He shrugs in a boyish way. "I can be superfast when motivated. I see that you also showered." He looks pointedly at my wet hair.

"It was an in-and-out situation. I can't go to class smelling like sex again."

His gaze turns smoldering hot. "If you don't want a repeat of that, don't tease me."

It's not exactly the *über*dark reaction I'm used to from him, but it's not overly sweet either. I can deal with that.

He takes my hand, lacing his fingers with mine.

"What are you doing?" My voice rises an octave.

"Making sure no punk gets any ideas about you."

More like marking his territory. I told him I don't belong to anyone, but the stupid butterflies in my stomach don't care. They're having a rave in celebration.

"Who is getting ideas about me?" I ask.

"Justice, for starters."

I groan. "Please, do not remind me of that jackass. I need to keep him away from Sage, but I don't know how."

"Easy peasy. Let Luke handle him."

I shake my head. "I can't tell him anything. Sage would never forgive me."

Jason looks at me. "Do you want to save her from a predator or not?"

"He's shady, but we don't know if he's a predator."

"He's eighteen and going after a naive sixteen-year-old. What the hell do you think he is?"

"Okay, fine. But letting Luke loose on his ass is not going to help. Sage has a huge crush on Justice, so the more we tell her he's bad news, the more she'll want him. You know, the forbidden fruit appeal."

Thanks to the conversation, I don't realize we've crossed into the main school building until the buzz of the student body surrounds us. Everyone turns to stare at Jason and me, making me self-conscious—and wary. In the land of cell phones and social media, all it takes is one upload of a photo of me to lead Juan straight here. Disguise or not, now that he knows I'm alive, he'll be on the lookout.

Maybe I secretly do wish that he'll find me, so I can stop living this lie. What other explanation is there for dating the king of the school?

Wait? Is that what's happening? Am I Jason's girlfriend? Or maybe that's the next level of his twisted game. Make everyone —including me—believe that we're a couple. And then he'll do something awful to humiliate me.

He sees Finn and Luke and veers straight toward them.

Luke is the first to notice our joined hands. Smiling, he says, "Ah, isn't love great?"

Finn twists his face into a "what the fuck" expression that'd be priceless if it wasn't aimed at me. Then he stares at Jason with a question in his eyes, which doesn't get acknowledged.

"Jesus fucking Christ," someone exclaims near us.

It's Cameron, who is staring bug eyed at my hand in Jason's. "I heard the rumors, and I couldn't believe it. So I had to see it for myself."

Finn rolls his eyes. "Quit being so fucking dramatic, Cam."

"I called it, didn't I, Nicola?" Luke winks at me, smiling from ear to ear.

"I don't understand what's the big deal. We're just holding hands," I say.

"Ignore them. They're immature babies," Jason pipes up.

"I have to get to class." I try to pull my hand free, but he holds it tighter.

"I'll walk with you."

My face is in flames by the time we walk away from his friends and cousin.

"Is this show really necessary?" I ask when we stop in front of my classroom.

"What do you mean, Nicola? You don't like to be seen with me?" His eyes are widely innocent, but the corners of his lips are upturned.

"Come on, Jason. I wasn't born yesterday. You don't simply stop hating someone so fast, no matter how good the sex is."

He pulls me to him, trapping my hands behind my back so there's no space between our bodies. He brings his mouth close to my ear and whispers. "Aren't you being a bit cocky? You don't know if I think fucking you is that good."

I turn my face to his, bringing our lips only inches apart. "The bulge in your pants says you do. It tells me you want to fuck me right now."

His eyes turn into nothing but slits. "Careful now, sweetheart. I told you not to tease me."

A throat clearing behind us forces Jason to pull back.

I turn to find Mr. Kaufman standing there with a scowl etched on his face. "Are you coming in or not, Ms. Devlin?"

"Of course, sir."

My cheeks are burning up, but I'm still grinning when I pass Mr. Kaufman. I rattled Jason and left him hanging without a chance to retaliate. I know it'll come later, but I'm not afraid. Whatever Jason has planned for me won't work to bring me down, because it seems I love when he hates me.

26

NICOLA / ISABELLE

*T*he one-eighty change in Jason's attitude is enough distraction for me to ignore the looming threat of Juan. I don't know if he did it by design so I wouldn't freak out and run away, or if he's up to something. I'll try my best not to be swept away by this other side of him, but it's hard to keep my shields up when my heart beats faster every time he's near.

"A penny for your thoughts." He hugs me from behind and kisses my shoulder.

He spent the night in my room again, even though it's against school policy. The rules of student conduct exist only to appease the parents and are rarely enforced. It was the same way in my previous school.

"I'm just thinking that I have to start getting ready soon."

"Ready to go where?"

"I've made plans with Sage."

"Are you going to tell me what those plans are?"

I roll over so I can see his face. "Why do you want to know?"

He holds my stare but remains silent for a moment. "I'll feel better if I know where you'll be."

My heart skips a beat. How am I going to protect myself from him when he says things like that? "Because of Juan."

His gaze hardens. "That's one reason."

"There's more than one?" I raise an eyebrow. "Let's hear the others, then."

He grimaces and then turns onto his back to stare at the ceiling. "Don't ask me to explain things I don't understand myself."

I lean on my forearm, resting my head against my fist. "Are you catching feelings, Jason Novak?"

My statement was meant as a tease, but he scowls and swings his legs off the side of the bed, getting up.

"I was joking." I sit up.

"Whatever. I also have shit to do."

I've never seen him get dressed so fast. I would be lying if I said his reaction didn't hurt. He walks out without a word or second glance, banging the door hard. I'm left reeling without a clue what's gotten into him.

Isn't it obvious, Isabelle? You just got him to show his hand. His devoted boyfriend act was all a bunch of BS.

I'm glad that I managed to get him to reveal his true colors, even if it was by accident. But I'm disappointed that I was right all along.

Feeling less enthusiastic about my day, I jump out of bed and head for the shower. I'll give myself permission to wallow in misery for a moment, but I'd better change my attitude by the time I'm ready to see Sage.

I MEET Sage in front of Dennis's Diner, since I'm not familiar with all the stores in Triton Cove yet. She's wearing a cute yellow sundress that makes her look younger than sixteen.

The conversation I had with Jason about Justice comes to the forefront of my mind. If Justice had good intentions toward her, he wouldn't act sneakily. I have to do something. Maybe steering her toward a boy her age is the way to go, but I don't know anyone that fits the bill, save for Luke's friends, and I doubt he'd approve of them either.

"Hi, Sage. You look so pretty!" I greet her with a smile.

"Oh, thanks." She blushes and glances at her dress. "Believe it or not, this was a gift from Luke."

My jaw drops. "Wow, he has good taste."

"Yeah."

"So where do you want to go first?"

"There's a secondhand shop that has really cool dresses just around the corner."

"Awesome. I love those stores."

"Me too. Most of the girls at Maverick Prep turn up their noses when I say I buy most of my clothes secondhand. I don't care what they think though."

"Good for you. I confess I get most of my stuff online these days."

For reasons I really can't tell her.

"I think that's what most people do. Let's find something amazing for you to wear tonight."

"Tonight?"

She tilts her head. "For Jason's party."

My cheeks become warm. "Oh, I'm not going to that."

"Why not? Aren't you dating? I know you said you weren't invited, but I thought dating him changed things."

Her question rekindles the emotion I felt earlier when Jason stormed out of my room. "I don't know if we are. But anyway, I still wasn't invited." I shrug, trying to sound nonchalant.

She narrows her gaze. "That sucks."

"Not rea—"

A guy rushes out of the convenience store to our right and bumps into Sage, sending her to the ground. She falls on her butt, and the momentum almost sends him down too.

"Dude, watch where you're going," I say.

"Oh my God. I'm so sorry," he tells Sage, ignoring me. He offers his hand and helps her back on her feet. "Are you okay?"

Her cheeks are flushed when she says, "I'm okay. Don't worry."

"I didn't see you," he continues.

I bite my tongue as I notice her reaction. She's blushing even more furiously now under his attention. Maybe because he's a hottie.

"Eric, what in the world?" An older man walks out of the store. "What did I say about running around like a maniac?"

The guy rubs the back of his neck, looking sheepish. "Sorry, Grandpa."

"Are you okay, young lady?" the man asks Sage.

"I'm fine."

"Eric, go grab a couple of water bottles for the girls."

"Yes, sir."

"Oh, you don't need to bother," Sage replies, but Eric heads back into the convenience store anyway.

"It's the least he can do after running over you," the man replies.

Eric returns a moment later and hands over cool water bottles to Sage and me.

"Thanks," I say.

Sage seems frozen and simply stares at Eric. I elbow her arm, which snaps her out of it. "Yes, thank you."

"No problem. See you around," he says, and then runs across the street.

His grandfather shakes his head, making a disapproving sound in the back of his throat. "Learned nothing."

"Well, we should get going," I say. "Thanks for the water."

"No problem. You have a wonderful day." He waves and goes inside.

I wait until we put some distance between us and the store to ask, "Who was that guy?"

"I don't know. I've never seen him before."

"He's cute."

Sage's face becomes bright pink again. "He is? I didn't notice."

Didn't notice my ass. "Do you think he's a local?"

"Maybe."

"We need to find out where he goes to school."

"Why? Are you trying to get over Jason?"

Ah hell. I guess she could mistake my comment as an interest in the guy. "Oh, he's not for me. A bit too young. I was thinking maybe *you* would like to see him again."

Her expression closes off. *Shit, I went too far.*

"I don't think so." She stops suddenly and announces, "This is it."

Grumbling because of my failed attempt to make Sage forget Justice, I follow her in. Inside is a bit of a mess. There are tables of different sizes, heights, and shapes covered with all sorts of accessories and pieces of clothing. Against the walls, the racks are filled to the brim with colorful gowns, tops, and pants. It seems there's no rhyme or reason to the organization here.

"Wow. Where do we start?" I ask.

"Welcome to Alice's Closet. How can I help you?" a friendly sales assistant greets us from behind the counter.

"We're looking for evening gowns," Sage replies.

"Oh, you're lucky. I just received a shipment from LA. They're from an editorial shoot, so they're amazing."

She walks around the counter and guides us to the back of the store, where gowns hang from a mobile rack.

"Aren't they gorgeous?" She beams.

"Yeah," Sage replies absentmindedly, already distracted by the chiffon, tulle, and silk.

"Let me know if you want to try any on."

"We will, thank you," I say.

Sage pulls a sheer bright-red gown with gorgeous embroidered flowers on it from the rack and holds it against my body. "This would look stunning on you."

I try not to grimace. Red is my favorite color, but I can't wear it now. It'd be like wearing a neon sign. "It's lovely, but I don't need a dress."

"Would you at least try it? For me?" she pleads.

"Fine." I take the gown from her. "But we're shopping for you."

"I know." She keeps browsing until she finds a light-blue chiffon dress that would make her look like Arwen from *Lord of the Rings*.

"I *love* that," I say.

"Me too."

We both head to the dressing rooms, and when I see Sage wearing hers, I know she's found the one. She's glowing.

"Nicola, you look amazing. You need to get that."

"No, no. I said I'd try it on to indulge you. I can't wear red. It's not me," I lie.

She takes her phone from her purse and snaps a picture.

"What are you doing?" I say, panicking. "Don't post that to social media."

"Relax. I'm just texting Luke."

"Why would you do that?"

She smiles like the Cheshire cat. "Because I need his help convincing you to come to Jason's party with us."

Glowering, I cross my arms over my chest. "I'm not going to crash his party."

"It's not his party. It's his mother's."

"Even worse. I've met the woman, and she's a witch."

"Who's a witch?" Luke asks, sporting a broad smile.

"What are you doing here?" I ask, then glance at Sage. The little traitor. She must have told her brother where to find us.

"I was in the neighborhood." He gives me an elevator glance and wolf whistles. "Looking good, Nicola. Jason will eat his heart out when he sees you."

"I'm not getting the dress or going to the stupid party."

His wide eyes tell me he's genuinely surprised. "Why not? Everyone who matters will be there."

"Newsflash. I don't matter, hence I didn't get an invitation," I grit out.

"Bullshit. You *do* matter, or Jason wouldn't have looked in your direction."

"I know why Sage wants me to go, but why do you care?"

"Er…"

"My brother loves conflict, that's why. He thinks if you crash the party, something spectacular will happen."

I put my hands on my hips. "Oh, so I'm supposed to be his entertainment?"

He rubs the back of his back. "How is that such a terrible thing? You're a violinist. Isn't that entertainment?"

I open and shut my mouth, unable to come up with a retort. He got me.

"Sloane will be there, and she'll be all over Jason," Sage pipes up.

"For someone with such an angel face, you sure are a scheming little devil," I grumble.

Her eyes round. "I'm not a devil. I'm being a good friend."

An idea pops in my head, but I don't want Luke to hear it.

I turn to him. "Can you give us some privacy, please?"

"I'll wait outside, but you'd better buy that dress."

I shake my head as I watch him leave.

"What did you want to tell me that my brother couldn't hear?" Sage asks.

"I'll buy the dress and go to the party under one condition."

"Okay?"

"We have to find out where Eric goes to school and come up with a plan for you to properly meet him."

Her mouth becomes a perfect O. "You're insane."

"I'm not. I saw the way you checked him out."

"I didn't!"

"Come on, Sage. What's the harm? He's cute, and you can't go wrong with a guy who respects his grandfather."

She furrows her brows and pouts. "Is that the only way you'll agree to come to the party with us?"

"Yep," I say, trying my best to contain my satisfied grin.

"All right."

I punch the air with my fist. "Yes!"

I'm so excited that I don't have time to worry that I'll be venturing into the viper's nest again.

27

NICOLA / ISABELLE

I learned my lesson from the last time I came to Victoria Petrov's house. So instead of catching a ride with Luke and Sage, I drove my own car. Naturally, Sage was suspicious, so she made her brother drive all the way to campus so I would follow them.

Once I give my car keys to the valet, I find the duo waiting by the front steps. Sage looks even more beautiful tonight with her dark hair French braided in the front, and the rest cascading loose in soft curls. Luke in a tux is quite the sight. He looks like a rogue spy who's about to wreak havoc at any moment.

"You clean up nice." He gives me an appreciative smile.

"Uh, thanks?"

I run my hands over the embroidery on the flowy skirt. The dress is mostly see-through aside from the strategically placed flowers embroidered throughout the piece. Even the corset is sheer. The skirt is lined, but the lining stops above the knee.

"I could have met you here, you didn't need to escort me," I continue.

"And risk you not coming at all?" Sage raises an eyebrow.

"There's also the issue that you're technically not on the guest list," Luke chimes in. "So we have to sneak you in."

I grimace. I haven't thought about that. "Great."

"Don't worry. It'll be a piece of cake." He beams wickedly.

Now that I'm here, I don't want to suffer the humiliation of being denied entrance. So I raise my chin and portray the attitude that I belong. There's a couple of security personnel checking names at the entrance—let's hope I can convince them.

"Luke, Sage, and Claire Halle," Luke tells the guy.

Who the hell is Claire Halle?

The man is serious as he glances at his screen, then he nods. "Enjoy your evening, sir, ladies."

I wait until we're out of earshot to stop Luke and ask, "Who's Claire?"

"Our mother. She won't be here tonight," he says as he scans ahead.

"Who are you looking for, Luke?" Sage follows his line of sight.

With a closed-off expression, he replies, "No one. Let's find Nicola's boyfriend. I don't want to miss that."

"He's not my boyfriend," I grit out.

I'm already regretting coming to this party. Talk about looking desperate. We don't manage to walk beyond the grand entry foyer when Jason's voice echoes behind us.

"What are you doing here?"

JASON

I STAY in my childhood room for as long as I can, but when soft music and chatter breach the closed doors, I know it's time to face the lions. I head downstairs, fighting not to loosen my tuxedo tie. I stop midstep when I see Isabelle at the bottom of the grand staircase, looking like a goddess in red. My heart speeds up and the world seems to go off-kilter. I reach for the railing, afraid that my legs will desert me.

"What are you doing here?" I ask when I make it to the bottom stair.

She turns slowly, and instantly, I know I said the wrong thing.

"Nicola came with us." Luke stops next to her, smiling like a fiend.

I notice that Sage is right behind him. *Shit.* He did this on purpose, because seeing things go up in flames is his favorite pastime. I'd knock that smile off his face in any other circumstance, but Isabelle turns on her heel and heads for the door.

"Nicola, wait." I rush after her and grab her arm.

"I know when I'm not welcome, Jason," she seethes.

"I didn't say you weren't. I was just surprised."

"You didn't invite me."

My brows rise. "I had nothing to do with the guest list, and considering how well things went the last time you were here, I didn't think you'd want to come."

It's not a complete lie. I didn't want her here because she's making me feel things I'm not ready to face. Case in point—my reaction at seeing her.

The rage disappears from her gaze, but the hurt stays in place. "It's better if I leave anyway."

She's right. It would be better if she left, but now that she's here, I don't want her to go. "No. You're staying."

"Why?"

I step closer and touch her hair. She braided it to one side, and loose wisps frame her face. I wish she wasn't wearing those hideous brown lenses though, but even with them, she takes my breath away.

"Because if you go, I'll have to follow you."

She shakes her head. "I'm tired of playing this game with you, Jason."

"This is not a game, not anymore." Unable to restrain myself, I cup her cheek and kiss her lips softly. I take it as a win that she doesn't step back.

"Aww. You guys are so sweet," Luke chimes in.

I step back and flick my gaze to him. "You'd better stay out of my way tonight, punk."

His eyes turn round. "Wait? Are you mad?" He shakes his head. "That's the payment I receive for playing Cupid."

Sage tugs his arm. "Come on, Luke. Leave them alone."

They finally walk away, and now I can properly enjoy Isabelle's company.

"You look stunning tonight," I tell her.

Her cheeks turn bright pink, and she glances down. "Thanks. You do have Luke and Sage to thank. They convinced me to get this dress and come to the party."

"I'll thank Sage. I'll think about Luke." I take her hand, and for the first time, I don't know what to say.

"So… what happens next?" she asks.

The first thought that comes to my mind is to whisk her to my room and let her ride me while wearing that dress. But that's a fantasy I can't indulge right now. "We mingle. Come on."

With my hand firmly clasping hers, I steer her to the outside area where most of my mother's guests are. And then comes the performance. I become a different person in front of these snobby motherfuckers. They're the most important and influential people in Triton Cove, and they're as fake as they can be.

The first time I introduce Isabelle as my girlfriend, she tenses. I didn't plan on doing it, it just came out and it turns out, I don't mind the idea at all.

"I'm your girlfriend now? Thanks for the heads-up," she says under her breath when we get a reprieve in introductions.

"I figured it'd be easier. But I can introduce you as my delicious fuck bunny if you prefer," I joke.

And it goes right over her head, if her glower is any indication.

"Relax, babe. I was kidding."

Finn spots us and makes a beeline in our direction. "Dude, where have you been?" he asks, not hiding his sour mood.

"I was biding my time. Why suffer these sycophants longer than necessary?"

"I've been here for half an hour and already had my fill of them." He glowers in his parents' direction.

"Hi, Finn, nice to see you," Isabelle greets him in a sarcastic tone.

He grimaces. "Hey, Nicola. Sorry, these parties bring out the worst in me. You look pretty."

"Thank you. You look... different."

He tilts his head. "How so?"

"I guess it's the tux and the fact your wild hair is bound for once."

He reaches for his low ponytail. "Not my choice. My father insisted."

"Ah yeah, that has Uncle Florian's fingers all over it," I chime in.

"So you guys are official now?" he asks.

"Yep." I bring Isabelle's hand to my lips and kiss the back of it.

"Do *not* introduce her to my father if you don't want your evening ruined."

"I don't think he can say worse things than Victoria did," Isabelle replies, making my stomach churn.

I never learned what Mom told her while I was *fetching* my violin.

Finn's attention diverts to something behind us. "Cam is here, and… ah hell, he's making his way to Halsey's parents. I gotta run interference." He sprints away before we can say anything.

Isabelle looks over her shoulder and asks, "Who's Halsey?"

"We'd better not get into that story now. It's long, and I don't know all the details."

From the corner of my eye, I notice Grandpa making his way toward us. Shit. He's not the worst of the Novak family, but I don't need him giving Isabelle the third degree.

"My grandfather is coming our way. I'd better go see what he wants. Why don't you get something to drink? I'll find you."

Her eyebrows squinch together, and I expect a *no* from her, but then she surprises me. "Okay, sure."

I drop her hand fast and forgo kissing her on the cheek—even though I really do want to. If Grandpa witnesses any PDA, he won't leave me alone. But I can't help looking over my shoulder to check on her before I reach him.

She's gone.

28

NICOLA / ISABELLE

*J*ason doesn't want me to meet the rest of his family. I understand his reasons, and a small part of me is thankful. But there's a side of my brain—the stupid one—that's annoyed that he's trying to hide me from them.

I refuse to show him or anyone else who might be watching that I'm bothered. I spin on my heel and stride toward the bar set up by the pool.

"Good evening, miss. What would you like?" the bartender asks me.

"One cubata, please," I request without thinking.

This reminds me so much of Juan. Why did my brain default to that? When the bartender places the drink in front of me, I stare at it, frozen.

"What's the matter, Nicola? Did Jason abandon you already?" Sloane stops next to me.

I didn't notice her presence until she spoke. To hide my

nervousness, I grab the drink and take a big sip. Mercifully, the taste doesn't trigger a panic attack.

"He's only playing with you. That's what he does, and considering how he's always hated you, I wonder how dumb you can be, to believe he flipped."

Fucking hell. When it rains, it pours. I don't want to deal with catty women right now. "You should have worn green instead of black to match your jealousy." I walk around her, or at least I try.

She grabs my arm, digging her long fake nails in my skin. "I know there's something fishy going on between you and Jason, and I *will* find out what it is, Nicola."

I pull free from her grasp, ready to tell her to fuck off, when Victoria Petrov walks over.

"Nicola Devlin, what a surprise, seeing you at my party."

If she mentions I wasn't invited in front of Sloane, I'm going to die of shame. It's already hard to pretend Sloane's threat to unveil the secret that ties me to Jason has not rattled me. With Juan actively looking for me, I can't let the hateful bitch find out who I am.

"I'm surprised myself," I say.

"Hello, Mrs. Novak," Sloane pipes up.

The shy smile she's sporting now makes me want to roll my eyes. *Could she lay the sweet act on any thicker?*

Victoria whips her face in her direction as fast as a cobra. "It's *Ms. Petrov.*"

Sloane's shoulders slouch forward, and she seems to become smaller. I'd feel bad for her if I were nicer. But I have no sympathy for snakes.

Victoria immediately dismisses Sloane's presence and returns her attention to me. "Since you're here, how about I give you a tour of the house, Nicola?"

"Uh, sure. That'd be nice."

Victoria laces her arm with mine as if we're old friends. My skin breaks out in goose bumps as the feeling I'm getting cozy with the devil takes over. I crane my neck, hoping to find Jason in the crowd. The last thing I want is to spend time alone with his mother. I don't trust her friendliness one bit.

"I understand that you and my son are an item now," she says.

"Uh, yeah, it's new."

She veers for the stairs. I guess we're starting the tour on the second floor, where no one can witness it if she decides to kill me. My pulse accelerates, even though I know the biggest threat Victoria presents is to hurt me with words. Still, dots of sweat form on my forehead.

"Jason has never dated anyone seriously. You must be something special." Sarcasm drips from her two-forked tongue.

I don't know how to reply to that without sounding conceited. If she only knew how fucked up my relationship with Jason is, maybe she wouldn't bother with this farce.

Once on the second floor, we pass several closed doors in the hallway and stop in front of none. As far as tours go, this is a strange one.

"Jason has always been peculiar, especially as a child. Too sensitive. He didn't inherit the Petrov backbone."

"I don't think being sensitive is a detriment," I say.

She chuckles. "It is when you're destined to be on top. But you wouldn't know that, would you, honey?"

We finally stop in front of a closed door at the end of the corridor.

"Alas, his whiny phase didn't last long, but he decided to pick up an even more disturbing habit." She opens the door and says, "Go on, dear. Have a look."

I hesitate. "What's in there?"

"This is Jason's former practice room. I think you should know what you're getting into."

I'm leery about going into dark rooms, so I turn on the lights first. It takes only two steps forward for me to understand Victoria's reason for bringing me here. The walls in the room are papered from top to bottom with pictures and news articles about me.

My heart is beating so loud, it sounds like a stampede. She knows who I am.

"What's this?"

"This, my dear, is why I thought Jason would never be interested in any girl."

"I don't understand."

"My son has a pathological obsession with Isabelle Maldonaro, a prodigy violinist who sadly died a year ago."

I swallow the huge lump in my throat and come closer to one of the walls. There are newspaper articles dating back to eight years ago. But what catches my attention—maybe because it's the biggest printout—is the announcement of my death. I feel sick and dizzy, and I have the sensation the walls are caving in. I knew he hated me, but this looks like the room of a serial killer. It reminds me of the room Juan locked me in, which had walls covered by photographs of us together. Have I gotten involved with another crazy asshole?

No, it's much worse. I think I've fallen for one. I hug my middle, trying to control the shakes that are wreaking havoc in my body.

"Mother, what's going on?" Jason asks from the door.

"I was just showing Nicola your old practice room," she replies sweetly.

I turn around, and when my gaze connects with his, my entire world crumbles. His eyes are guilty as hell. I can't keep it together. I have to leave, or I'll do something insane, such as rip all those photos of me from the wall.

I push him out of my way and don't stop running.

29

JASON

I turn to my mother as rage simmers in my gut, low and dangerous. "What have you done?"

"I thought it was only right to show Nicola what she's getting into. No woman should start a relationship with a guy who's obsessed with a dead girl."

Curling my hands into fists, I take a menacing step toward her. "You had no right."

Her gaze narrows to slits. "I have every right in the world. This is my house. If you didn't want anyone to know about your sickness, you should have pulled all this shit down when Isabelle died."

I can't waste my time trying to understand my mother's motives. I have to go after Isabelle and explain to her I'm not a psychopath like her ex.

"When I thought you couldn't sink any lower…" I grit out. "I can't deal with you right now. I have to go after Nicola."

I start for the door, but my mother gets in my way. "You're not going after anyone. You have to play soon."

A crazy laugh bubbles up to my throat. "You must be out of your goddamned mind if you think I'm going to perform for your fucking guests."

Her blue eyes spark with rage, and the hard slap to my face comes a second later. "You will *not* disrespect me, Jason. Now grab your violin and get ready."

My ears are ringing from the hit, and my cheek burns, but she could beat me senseless and I still wouldn't play. "I'm sorry, Mother, but my years of bowing to your whims are over."

The urge to shove her out of my way is enormous, but I won't stoop to her level and resort to violence. I walk around her instead and then sprint down the hallway and stairs. In the entry foyer, I have the misfortune to bump into Sloane and her friends.

"Jason, I was look—"

"Not now, Sloane." I rush out of the house, but I don't see Isabelle anywhere.

I ask one of the valets if he's seen her, and he tells me she just left. She wised up; she drove her own car tonight.

My car is in the garage, which is currently blocked by all the other vehicles.

"I need a car," I tell the valet.

"Sir?" The guy looks at me like I've lost my mind.

"Don't fucking 'sir' me. Give me the car that's closest to the exit. I'm Victoria Petrov's son."

Dropping my mother's name does the trick. The guy grabs a fob from his stash and runs down the driveway. He returns a minute later, driving a Maserati Levante SUV. I have no idea who this car belongs to, but it's fast, and that's all I care about.

Traffic is nonexistent on the way back to campus, but as fast as I drive, I don't see Isabelle's car on the road. The valet must have lied about the time she actually left the party. In the dorm's garage, I see that her car is there. Naturally, I head straight to her dorm room, but I knock first, because bursting in will not do me any favors.

"Isabelle, please open up," I plead.

She doesn't answer.

Hell. I use my master key then, because I can't simply wait for her to calm down. That might never happen and she's a flight risk. I find her room empty though.

What the hell. Where did she go?

A quick search of her room tells me she didn't pack up and leave, but the violin I gave her is missing. On a hunch, I head to the main school building. The master key also works there, but the issue is the new alarm system they installed. They change the passcode every week, and I haven't bothered to get the new one yet. There are other ways to gain entrance, though.

I circle the perimeter until I find one of the security guards.

"Hey, Jonas." I wave at him.

"Jason. I would ask what you're doing here, but judging by your attire, I can guess."

"What do you mean?"

"You're looking for your girlfriend, right? Pretty girl wearing a red dress?"

"Yes, have you seen her?"

"I just let her in. I normally wouldn't, but she looked distressed and begged to use the music room. I can't stand to see a girl cry."

"She was crying?"

He nods. "You'd better get in there and make things right."

"I will, thanks, Jonas." I reach inside my pocket and fish out a hundred-dollar bill.

He thanks me and then types in the code to open the side door into the building. I sprint to the music room before the door shuts again. Music has filled the silent corridor, but it's not the violin I hear, it's the piano.

I skid to a halt. The music room door is ajar, and I can see that Isabelle is indeed playing the piano… and she's terrific at it. I'm not surprised. I think she could play every single instrument in an orchestra exceptionally.

She doesn't glance in my direction when I finally enter the room, but she's aware I'm there. I don't say a word, just listen to her play for a moment. My fingers itch to create music though, so when I spot her violin case propped against a chair, I don't think twice, I head straight for it.

Isabelle doesn't miss a beat when I join her with the worst-sounding instrument known to man. How the hell did she manage to produce anything decent with this? It sounds like nails scratching a blackboard at first. But eventually, I find my groove, and my ears don't suffer anymore. The music reaches a crescendo, and then it ends.

She keeps her fingers on the keys, breathing hard, but she still won't look at me. My heart is constricted painfully. The only time I felt such agony before was when I thought she had died. I don't know how I didn't come to the realization sooner. It's always been obvious what my true feelings for her are.

I lower the violin and walk over.

She glances at me, and I get proof that Jonas didn't lie about her crying. Her eyes are red, and it's not because of her contact lenses. She took them off at some point.

"You were right about this." I lift the violin in my hand. "It sucks."

She doesn't blink as she stares at me in silence for a long stretch.

"Why the piano?" I ask.

Ignoring my question, she asks one of her own. "What do you want, Jason?"

"I want to explain what you saw."

She jumps from the stool and steps away from me. "What is

there to explain? How long have you been collecting all that stuff about me?"

"Does it matter? I know anything I tell you now won't help my case. But there was a time when I didn't hate you, Isabelle. You were my idol."

Her face twists into something akin to pain, and her eyes become brighter. "It doesn't matter. What I saw all over your walls paints a pretty clear picture of your twisted mind."

I try not to wince, but her words hurt like punches.

"I'm fucked up. I don't deny that. But my hatred for you was just an excuse. You were my scapegoat for all the shit that has happened in my life. I have little faith that you'll understand or forgive me."

"Good. I'm glad you don't have unrealistic expectations."

So this is what it feels like to fall and shatter to pieces. My mother's plan worked perfectly. There's no chance in hell Isabelle will choose to stay with me. She barely escaped a psychopath alive. I bet I don't look much different than that motherfucker right now.

"I won't stop you from leaving Triton Cove if that's what you want, but before you go, I want you to listen to something I composed."

Her eyebrows scrunch together. "Why?"

I curl my lips into a crooked grin, hoping she can't see my pain. "Please, indulge me."

"Will you stop harassing me if I do?"

"Cross my heart and hope to die."

She shakes her head, and then drops on the stool again as if the conversation tired her out. "Fine. Go on."

My heart is thumping like an Irish dancer, and my mouth is suddenly unbearably dry.

"I composed it the week before the competition in Switzerland eight years ago. I wanted to play it there, but my mother forbade it."

171

Isabelle doesn't ask me the reason. Having met my mother, she can guess.

I haven't played this in a long time, but I haven't forgotten the notes. My hands are clammy, and the butterflies in my stomach take me back to the moment before I was about to meet Isabelle for the first time. I stop the memory from taking complete shape in my mind, or I'll lose my bravado.

When the first notes echo in the room, it hurts more than I thought possible. I can't hold her stare, so I close my eyes and try to forget that my world is crumbling, that the girl I spent half my life worshipping and then hating is now beyond my reach.

The irony is not lost on me. I had to lose any chance I had with her to realize I've been in love with her all this time.

The song is only three minutes long, but it seems like an eternity has passed when I finish. I lower the violin and take a deep breath before I dare to look at her again. And she's in tears.

"Was it that bad?"

She shakes her head. "No. It was beautiful."

"I wrote it for you. You were the muse."

Her body shakes as she releases a shuddering breath. "What did I do to you to change how you felt about me?"

Unable to hold her stare, I glance at the poster on the wall behind her. "You treated me like shit."

"What? I wouldn't do that to anyone."

"Well, you did to me. I came to see you right before you were about to perform. I could tell you were nervous, so I said you had nothing to worry about because you were perfect."

I flick my eyes to her again. She's staring at me, wide eyed, as if I were telling a story about someone else.

"You started yelling, called me a filthy liar, and then shoved me against the wall before storming off. I was so shaken that when it was my time to perform, I fucked up royally. Not only did I not win an apprenticeship with Carlos Ferrera, I became a joke. I couldn't get into any important program afterward."

Her expression crumples, and then she hides behind her hands. "Jason, I'm so sorry. I have no memory of that."

"I know now that you don't."

She looks at me again. "How do you know? I could be lying."

"But you aren't. I get it now. You were probably having a nervous breakdown. It had nothing to do with me."

She gets up and walks over. I don't move even though I'm dying to pull her into my arms and crush my lips to hers.

She frames my face between her hands and stares deep into my eyes. "Thank you for that beautiful song."

"You're welcome. I guess this is the part where you say goodbye."

Frowning, she shakes her head. "I told you I'm done running."

"That doesn't mean a goodbye isn't imminent."

"Are you going to give up on me just like that?"

"This isn't a game to me anymore, Isabelle. I'm sorry you had to see that insane wall, I'm sorry I was so terrible to you when you got here. I'm letting you go without a fight because that's what you do when you love someone. You set them free."

She jolts back. "You love me?"

Shit. I can't believe I went all emo on her and confessed everything.

I grin. "Didn't your mother ever tell you that if a boy picks on you, it's because he secretly likes you?"

"No, she'd never say anything that stupid."

I shrug. "Well, it's true in my case."

She steps back, releasing my face. "I'm tired. Let's go home."

"Home?" I raise an eyebrow.

"My room." She lifts her hand. "Are you coming?"

30

NICOLA / ISABELLE

I'm trying to keep it together, but I'm screaming inside. I can't believe I treated Jason so horribly when we were younger. It doesn't justify his behavior, but now I understand his motives.

My mind is reeling, trying to process what happened this evening. From discovering his obsession to hearing him say he loves me, I don't know what to think or what to do about any of it.

His hand is still clasped in mine when I stop in front of my door. I fumble with the key thanks to the shaking. He takes it from me and unlocks the door. Our gazes lock, and I see in his eyes the same uncertainty that's swirling in my chest.

He waits for me to walk in first, and then follows, closing the door. "You haven't said a word since we left. What are you thinking about?"

I turn around and look at him. "I don't know. It's a lot to process."

He runs his fingers through his hair. "I know."

"Did you really mean it?"

"Mean what?" His brows arch.

I swallow the lump in my throat. I don't know why the jitters are getting the better of me. Maybe it's because I'm afraid this is all a lie. "Do you really love me?"

He walks over and stops short of invading my personal space. "Yes. I've never said that to anyone before."

"Me neither," I confess.

His eyes widen. "Not even *him*?"

I shake my head. "No. I couldn't bring myself to say it. I thought there was something wrong with me. Maybe I could never fall in love."

"Do you still believe that?"

My heart is running at the speed of light now. I could lie and say yes, but this time, it's the other way around, I can't bring myself to hide the truth.

"No." I touch his cheek and his eyes flutter closed for a moment. "Despite everything that has happened between us, I fell for you, Jason. I fell for you so hard that I don't know any more which way is up or down."

Shaky laughter escapes his lips. "Thank fuck."

He reaches for the back of my head, twisting his fingers around my hair as he lowers his lips to mine. My body catches fire, and my bones melt while I'm caught in the vortex of Jason's kiss. I grab onto his shoulders, needing the support before my legs give out from under me.

He flattens one palm against my collarbone, a gesture that's sweet and hot at the same time. Keeping my mouth locked to his, I peel his tuxedo jacket off. I'm in a hurry to get rid of all our clothes, but Jason doesn't seem to share the same urgency.

He pulls away and whispers against my lips, "Do you know

the first thought that crossed my mind when I saw you tonight?"

"No." I keep my gaze glued to his mouth, wondering if he'll let me resume the kiss.

"I wished I could take you to my room and let you ride me while wearing this dress." His fingers glide over my cleavage, leaving a trail of goose bumps behind.

I laugh as euphoria spreads through my veins like wildfire. "Is that what you want, Jason?"

He grabs my chin possessively and looks into my eyes. "It depends."

"On what?"

"On whether you care about what happens to it? I can't guarantee it will remain in one piece."

"I'm not usually attached to material things, but I think I'd like to preserve this particular dress." I turn around and look over my shoulder. "Help me unzip it?"

He kisses me between my shoulder blades and then runs his tongue down my back as he unzips the garment.

I gasp, reaching behind myself for him. The dress falls into a heap at my feet, and before I can move, he spins me around and covers one of my nipples with his mouth. Arching my back, I thread my fingers through his hair, yanking at the strands. He nibbles and sucks, driving me insane with longing. Breast play never did much for me, but Jason's tongue is pure magic.

He releases my nipple with a loud pop and trails open kisses up my neck to my ear.

"What do you want, Isabelle?" he whispers, and then bites my earlobe.

I melt into him, trying to remember how to speak.

"You," I murmur.

He chuckles, sending wisps of desire down my spine. "Your wish is my command, my love."

He leads me to the bed and nudges me to sit on the edge. I'm still wearing my panties, but Jason has most of his clothes on. Not breaking eye contact, he unbuttons his shirt slowly and then lobs it to the side. Unfortunately, there's another shirt underneath, which he keeps on.

"Still too many clothes." I pout.

"Patience, darling."

I narrow my eyes, knowing he's teasing me on purpose. Two can play at that game. I rub my thumb over my lips, and then I suck my middle finger. Jason's eyes bug out and then narrow. Now that my finger is thoroughly wet, I drag it down my belly until I reach the edge of my underwear.

"Oh no, sweetheart. You're not pleasuring yourself tonight." He drops to his knees and softly runs his hands over my thighs.

"You'd better do something about it quickly, then."

He parts my legs and, holding my stare, leans forward to lick my pussy through the fabric of my panties.

I gasp, then I moan. His tongue is torturous and sinful, and it's going to shatter me in no time. I reach for the back of his head, urging him to keep going.

He pulls the fabric aside and with one swipe of his tongue over my clit, he pushes me right off the edge.

"Oh my God, Jason." I pull his hair harder.

My body shakes from head to toe as a violent wave of pleasure levels me. I fall back on the mattress, my body turned into mush, keeping my eyes closed because the room is spinning out of control.

I hear him take off the rest of his clothes, and then his body covers mine. His erection presses against my belly as he nudges his nose against the crook of my neck.

"I love your taste when you come on my tongue," he whispers in my ear.

"I feel the same way. Slide off me and I'll return the favor."

"No, I want to come inside your sweet pussy first."

With a simple movement of his hips, his cock slides into

position, but he doesn't penetrate me at once. Instead, he teases me at my entrance while he kisses my neck.

"Jason, please. I thought you weren't going to be cruel anymore."

"I'm not, babe. I just know that once I'm inside you, I'm not going to last long."

I bring my knees up, hooking my legs at the ankle behind his ass. "I don't care. We have the whole night."

"When you put it that way…." He pushes forward, sheathing himself to the hilt.

His fullness stretching me makes me complete. I never knew one could feel this way during sex, but I never experienced anything like this before. I wasn't a virgin when I met Jason, but I might as well have been.

I lose the ability to speak or think, but it doesn't matter. I wouldn't be able to say a word, because Jason claims my mouth again while he fucks me hard and fast. I know this will take me to oblivion in no time, but I just hold on to him tight, knowing that my life with him will be the greatest ride.

31

JASON

*A*s expected, my mother blows up my phone the next day. I shut it off when it doesn't stop ringing. Isabelle stirs next to me, making the most delicious kitten sound that wakes up my cock. I kiss her shoulder, pulling her closer to me, and pressing my erection against her sweet ass.

"How can you have a hard-on after our all-night marathon?" she asks in a sexy, sleepy voice.

I dig my fingers into her hips. "Because it's you, and I'll never get my fill."

She rolls over, facing me. Her lips are still red and swollen from all the kissing, and her hair is a mess, but she's the most beautiful girl I've ever seen. She traces my hairline with the tips of her fingers, sending a shiver down my back.

"I can't believe this is real," she says.

"To be honest, me neither."

"I'm going to miss our hate sex though."

I laugh, not having expected that comment to come out of her mouth. "Is that so? We can always role-play."

She wrinkles her nose. "It's not the same thing, but...." She walks her fingers down my chest and keeps going south until they curl around my shaft. "I'm not opposed to some bedroom games."

"Hmm, what kind of games?"

The annoying sound of her phone ringing cuts off her reply. She tenses and begins to turn, but I wrap my arms around her waist. "Let it go to voice mail."

"I can't. That's the burner phone my parents use to contact me."

I release her at once. She jumps from the bed and hurries to her desk, where she takes the phone from her drawer. "Hello?"

Gone is the easygoing expression she had a moment ago. She begins to pace in front of me, and despite the lovely visual of her parading naked, her tense posture makes me forget any idea of sex.

"Yes, Mr. Cain told me. Are you okay?"

I can't hear the reply, so all I have to put the pieces together are her reactions.

"No, no one here knows about me." Her gaze flicks to mine. Guilt shines there. I suspect she's not used to lying to her folks. "I *am* being careful. I'm more concerned about you."

More silence follows, and then her face twists into a scowl.

"Mr. Cain has a big mouth. I'm not going to give up my passion because of Juan."

I guess her parents know she's playing at the recital. I agree it's risky, especially if video footage is posted online. But I won't stop her from doing something she loves because of that piece of shit. If he sets foot in Triton Cove, he'll wish he never had.

"Okay, I love you too. Bye."

Her eyes are dark like a summer storm when she glances at me.

"Let me guess. Your parents aren't keen that you're playing the violin again?"

"No. But they won't make me change my mind."

I get out of bed and walk to her. "He's not going to find you, and if he comes here, it will be the last thing he does in his miserable life."

She throws her arms around my neck and kisses me hard, taking me by surprise. I stagger back, not expecting her attack, but I recover in the next second. I grab her ass, lifting her off the floor. Her legs wrap around my hips, and her pussy rubs against my shaft, drawing a growl from me. I'm on fire again, but a bed won't do. There's too much raw energy between us; we might break the furniture.

I push her against the wall instead, and then guide my cock home. She bites my lower lip as I slam in and out of her. For a while the only sounds in the room are of pounding flesh and our combined moans and grunts. I don't even try to hold back and prolong the moment. As soon as she tightens around me and her body begins to shake, I let go of my restraint. We climax at the same time, and call me poetic and shit, but it's a beautiful thing.

WE USED the bed for the second morning round. Isabelle rolls to the side with a gasp, but I keep my hand nestled between her thighs as I try to catch my breath. She did most of the work this time on her knees, sucking my cock while I ate her pussy. I don't think I'll ever get tired of making love to her.

With my eyes still closed, I ask, "Are you okay, babe?"

"I will be in a minute, or ten."

We don't speak for several beats, but then I remember her reaction the first time we had sex and the memory is now nagging at me.

"Can I ask you a question?"

She turns on her side and looks at me. "Sure."

"Why did you get mad when I joked about you wanting to trap me with a baby?"

The levity leaves her gaze and sadness takes its place. *Shit. Way to spoil the morning, Jason.*

When she doesn't answer right away I add. "You don't need to tell me."

She swallows hard. "I guess now that we're together, you need to know." Her gaze drops to the mattress, clueing me in this will be a hard truth. "I can't have children."

Her answer feels like a punch to my chest. I can't breathe as I try to process her words. I have many questions, and all of them sound wrong in my head.

"Was it because of Juan?"

She nods, closing her eyes. I sit up and then pull her into my arms. "I'm going to kill him."

She eases back and meets my gaze straight on. "No, please promise you won't go after him."

I can't make that promise without lying. I run my fingers over her cheek. "I love you, and I promise I'll always protect you."

She hides her face in the crook of my neck, hugging me tighter.

"Let's stay in this room forever," I say.

"What about food? We can't keep doing this on an empty stomach."

In answer, my stomach growls, making her laugh. It's music to my ears after this grim revelation.

"See, your belly agrees." She tosses her legs to the side of the bed and gets up. "I'm taking a shower."

She's putting on a brave face for my benefit, and I play along because I don't want her trauma to stop her from being happy. "Do you want company?"

"Tempting, but I just want to stick to cleaning up."

I don't insist; I don't think I can do much right this second. I might need a couple of hours to recover. While I wait, I search for my phone and turn it back on. I can't remain cut off from the world only to avoid my mother. And I need a distraction from my dark thoughts.

She left several voice messages, which I'm sure contain all sorts of threats. I don't delete them, but I do ignore them for now. There's also a message from Reid, Finn's third musketeer, and it's in all caps.

REID: WHERE THE HELL ARE YOU, JERKFACE?

I frown at my phone and type a reply.

ME: I just woke up. Why are you yelling?
REID: You were supposed to meet me at the gym an hour ago.

Ah shit. I totally forgot that I asked Reid to help me this morning. I wasn't thinking clearly when I asked him yesterday to meet up this early on a Sunday. I also didn't expect to spend the night before fucking Isabelle. But this is too important to blow off.

ME: I'll be there in ten.

Most likely twenty, but he's already pissed. If I give him an accurate estimate, he'll leave. I jump from the bed and knock on the bathroom door.

"Hey, babe. Are you done?"

"Almost."

I push the door open just as she's turning the shower off.

"Wear comfortable clothes, preferably sweats or workout stuff."

She's frowning when she steps out of the stall. "Why? I thought we were going out for breakfast."

"Change of plans. I forgot I had made other arrangements for us."

She raises one eyebrow. "Are you going to tell me what they are?"

"Nope. It's a surprise."

I head for the shower and turn it back on. It feels good to be under the hot jets. Closing my eyes, I throw my head back and let the water hit my face. After a while, I have the sense I'm being spied on.

I turn and find Isabelle staring at me. A smile tugs the corners of my mouth. "Babe? You're supposed to be getting ready, remember?"

She blinks fast as if trying to snap out of a daze. "Then stop distracting me."

I laugh. "That's impossible."

She sticks her tongue out and then strides out of the bathroom. A minute later, I return to her room, wrapped in a towel. She's already dressed—thank fuck. I'd probably wanna go for a quickie otherwise. Guilt immediately spreads through my chest. How can I think about sex after what she told me?

Damn. I've never experienced this constant need to be with someone. Isabelle has put my libido into overdrive.

It just occurs to me I have nothing to wear save for yesterday's clothes, and we don't have time to stop by my room to change. It doesn't matter anyway. I'm not the one who'll be doing the training today.

In the hallway, Isabelle gives a quizzical look. "You aren't changing?"

"Nope. It's fine."

"Jason, what are you up to?"

I throw my arm over her shoulder. "It's nothing bad. I promise. Do you trust me?"

"Uh...."

"Ouch. Good grief, woman. Don't you know trust is the foundation of successful relationships?"

"Yeah, but it needs to be earned, and right now, you're acting pretty sus."

I can't argue with her there, but I don't want to disclose what we're doing beforehand. I'm not sure how she's going to react. The school allows athletes to use their facilities for training during the weekend, so we don't have to break in again.

On the way to the gym, I stop by a vending machine and grab us a couple of granola bars.

"Breakfast of champions," I tell her through a grin.

She scowls at the snack. "At least it's healthy. But I'd love some coffee too."

"I promise we'll go out for brunch, and you can have all the caffeine in the world."

We find a few people working out in the gym, but we're not here for the weight-lifting machines. I keep going until I reach one of the rooms. I hear grunts coming from inside, so that means Reid didn't bail.

"Who's in there?" Isabelle asks.

"Remember when I told you I wanted you to be ready in case Juan ever came after you?"

Her face becomes pale and her eyes bug out. "Yes."

"I've asked Reid to come in this morning to teach you some aikido moves. He's a black belt."

Her jaw drops. "Why didn't you tell me this before?"

I rub my neck. "I was afraid you wouldn't want to come."

Her expression is still pinched, so I'm not sure if she's mad or not.

"I... I don't know what to say."

"Don't worry. He doesn't know the reason."

"I'm not worried about that."

"Then why do you look like you're about to bust my balls?"

She shakes her head. "I'm not angry at you. I'm surprised and... touched." She rises on her tiptoes and kisses me softly on the lips.

"Good." I rest my hand on her hip and rub my thumb over the patch of exposed skin. Isabelle's eyes become hooded in a flash.

Jesus fucking Christ, Jason. Now is not the time to sex her up.

"We'd better go in. Reid has been waiting for over an hour," I say.

"Great. I hope he doesn't take that out on me."

Reid is giving the punching bag hell when we walk in. He sees us, but he's in the middle of a set of movements—or maybe he just wants to show off. He finishes his set with a roundhouse kick that's almost too fast to follow. Maybe I should get some lessons as well.

"Whoa," Isabelle blurts out.

Reid wipes off the sweat from his forehead and says, "Hello."

"I'm sorry we're late. I had no idea Jason had planned this session with you," she replies.

"I figured as much." He flips his gaze to mine, revealing his annoyance.

"Fair warning, I've never done martial arts," Isabelle continues.

Reid's gaze softens. "It's okay. I'll go easy on you. We're starting with the basics today. But I'll need a volunteer to demonstrate the moves."

He looks at me again and grins. His eyes glint with mischief. *Fuck.*

"Jason, if you'd be so kind as to join me on the tatami."

Ah hell. Here comes payback.

32

NICOLA / ISABELLE

The training session with Reid was interesting. I don't think I could perform any of the moves he taught me yet, but it was a start. All I know is that Reid made Jason pay for being late. When Monday morning comes, he's still limping.

"Are you okay?" I ask when he can't keep up with my pace.

"I'm fine," he grits out.

"Reid should have taken it easy on you. He could have broken your arm."

"Nah. He knows exactly how to inflict pain without maiming me. It's all good."

We stop at my locker first, and as I'm busy getting everything I need, Jason leans casually against the locker next to mine. "We need to get you a proper violin."

"I know. I'll keep looking online."

"No need. I think I found the perfect one for you."

I whip my face to him, frowning. "It'd better not be another unicorn explosion."

"No. It's an instrument worthy of a prodigy. Naturally, you need to try it out first."

"Where's the store?"

"In LA. The owner only deals with the best instruments in the world. I have a light schedule today. We could go after lunch."

I can't contain my enthusiasm. I'd consider blowing off the rest of my classes and going now, but I've already pushed my luck with Mr. Cain. He's not going to keep giving me a free pass just because of my secret and his friendship with my parents.

Behind me, someone shuts their locker with a bang. I turn, and surprise, surprise, it's Sloane. The glower aimed at us makes it clear she overheard our conversation.

"Man, she really hates my guts, doesn't she?"

"It's my fault. I've always known she had a thing for me. I shouldn't have led her on to make you jealous."

"I knew it!"

He steps closer, smiling like a fiend. "Just like I knew it bothered you to see me get up close and personal with another girl."

I curl my fingers around his jacket. "You'd better not pull that crap again."

He leans closer and nudges my neck with his nose. Desire spreads throughout my body, making me wish we were alone.

"I won't. Promise," he whispers.

"Get a room!" someone yells.

Jason tenses and looks at whoever spoke, ready to strike. It's Luke, smiling from ear to ear, who called us out.

"I don't know why you're grinning, punk. I haven't forgotten what you did last Saturday."

The amusement vanishes from his face. Finn and Cameron join their friend, but it's Finn who speaks next.

"We're leaving. Come on, Luke."

After they disappear in the crowd, I ask, "Why is everyone afraid of what Luke might do if he gets angry?"

"You haven't figured it out yet?"

I shake my head.

"Because he's a crazy motherfucker, that's why."

"But you're not afraid of him."

He smiles, and a gleam of danger shines in his eyes. "No, and you want to know why?"

"Sure." I shrug.

"I'm crazier than he is."

A shiver runs down my spine. I think that's what attracted me to Jason at first.

"Hmmm," I hum as my knees go weak. I'm fantasizing about him in the middle of the hallway, and I don't care.

His eyebrows furrow. "Hmmm? That's your response?"

I turn away from him and close my locker. "Let's go before we're late for class."

Or I combust on the spot.

TRITON COVE IS ONLY an hour from LA if you look at the distance on the map. But with the traffic, it takes us double the time to arrive. Only, I barely notice. It turns out that being locked in a car with Jason is not a bad thing, especially when his idea of passing time is to let his fingers have fun.

I'm blissfully relaxed when we arrive at our destination, but soon that's replaced by excitement. It seems being surrounded by exquisite instruments is also a turn-on for me. The store is large, and it has every instrument needed to create an orchestra. The grand pianos take central stage, naturally. I walk up to one and run my hand over the lid.

"I know my fingers are magic, but I have an inkling they aren't the reason for your goofy grin," he says.

"Guilty." I smile.

A bald man in his sixties approaches us. "Can I help you?"

"I believe you can. I'm Jason Novak. I called you about the Pedrazzini."

If possible, my excitement triples. My old violin was from the same Italian luthier.

The salesclerk's eyes widen. "Ah, of course. It's in storage. I'll be right back."

I wait until he's out of earshot to turn to Jason. "Why didn't you tell me? I honestly didn't think I could find another Pedrazzini."

"You shouldn't underestimate my connections, sweetheart."

The salesman returns with the violin in its case. With a flourish, he opens the lid.

My breath catches, and I swear I'm on the verge of crying. "It's beautiful."

"Would you like to play it?"

"Yes, please."

My hands are shaking as I take the violin out of its case.

"I also brought a bow by August Rau, if you would like to try it."

"Of course."

I feel like a kid on Christmas morning. I prop the violin on my shoulder but before I start, I lock gazes with Jason. He isn't smiling, but I know everything there is to know about his feelings just from the emotions shining in his eyes.

I decide to play the Romeo and Juliet solo, and soon I become lost in the music. I don't notice anything or anyone save for the broken boy who stole my heart. I'm not sure he knows that this is my way of saying I love him. I have yet to speak the words out loud.

When the music ends, my heart is beating furiously inside

my chest. My eyes are still locked with Jason's as I lower the violin.

"Sweet Mary, mother of God. That was beautiful," the salesman blurts out.

Blush spreads throughout my cheeks. "Thank you."

"If I didn't know any better, I'd say Isabelle Maldonaro was here."

My elation evaporates into thin air, and dread takes its place. "What?" I ask.

"The promising young violist who sadly passed away last year. I've never seen anyone play like her until now."

"You're too kind, sir." I lower my gaze, while I'm trying my best to not freak out.

The store's front door bangs loudly, making me jump. I glance at the window and see someone familiar speed away. *Shit.* It looks like Sloane. But it can't be. Why would she be here? Unless she followed us.

"We'll take the violin," Jason announces.

"Splendid." The salesman claps his hands.

I'm still in a daze and barely pay attention to what happens next. I don't even know how I get back into Jason's car.

"Are you okay?" he asks.

"No. He recognized me, Jason."

"He didn't, my love." He reaches for my hand and squeezes it tightly.

I pinch the bridge of my nose. "I think I saw Sloane at the store."

"What? Are you sure?"

"Not really. I was panicking. I could have imagined it."

Jason rubs his face. "I wouldn't put it past her to follow us here. She did overhear our conversation earlier."

"I didn't realize she was in love with you." I don't want to sound jealous, but I am.

"More like obsessed, judging by her actions."

"If she was at the store, then she heard what the sales guy said."

Jason clenches his jaw so hard that I can almost hear his teeth grind. "This is all my fault. I'm so sorry, babe."

I look out the window, not wanting him to see the tears gathering in my eyes. I'm more afraid for his safety than mine.

"It's not your fault," I reply in a small voice.

"If I hadn't said your real name in front of her, she wouldn't be suspicious."

"So what if she finds out? She doesn't know about the rest."

When Jason doesn't reply, I look at him, and I don't like what I see. His face is frozen in a cold and determined mask.

"What are you thinking?" I ask.

"Nothing."

"Jason, please don't lie to me."

He peels his eyes from the road for a moment. "I'm not. I'm honestly not thinking about anything in particular."

"I just don't want you to do something reckless."

"I won't. I promise. Do you trust me?" He grins.

I nod. "I trust you."

This time, I mean it.

33

JASON

*S*loane. *You fucking snake. I'm not going to let you endanger Isabelle.* I didn't lie to her in the car on the way back to Triton Cove. I wasn't thinking about anything specific besides berating myself for being such a moron.

I know Sloane too well. She doesn't have the patience to wait and attack when it will do more damage. Like clockwork, she finds me when I'm alone the next day at school.

"So the mystery is finally solved. Nicola is Isabelle Maldonaro."

I give her a droll look. "What do you want?"

She moves closer and runs her fingers down my jacket. "You know what I want."

I can't help my expression of disgust. "Really? Don't you have any self-respect?"

She laughs. "Get over yourself. I don't want to fuck you,

Jason. I want you and that little bitch to be miserable. Break up with her."

Rage quickly surges from the pit of my stomach. Sloane must think that dating Isabelle has made me soft. She needs to be reminded of who she's speaking to. "Are you sure you want to play that game with me, Sloane?"

Her eyes narrow. "I'm not afraid of you. If you don't do as I say, everyone will know who Nicola really is, and I bet she doesn't want that. No one fakes their own death without having a solid reason."

I laugh loudly like a lunatic. I even get tears in my eyes, not caring one bit that people are staring. Sloane doesn't know what to make of my reaction, and soon her bravado turns into uncertainty. And that's exactly how she should be feeling.

"Why the hell are you laughing? Do you think I'm joking?"

"You're either joking, or you're a dumb fuck." My amusement vanishes. "Someone with skeletons in their closet should never attempt blackmail, dear."

Her eyes widen. "I don't have any secrets. Nice try, Jason."

"Oh really. So you're saying you weren't fucking your sister's husband last summer?"

The blood seems to drain from her face. "What?"

I press my finger against my lips. "I wonder what Cassidy would think if she knew that while she was putting in long hours at the hospital to support that loser husband, her sister was sucking his cock instead of babysitting her nephews."

"You can't prove that," she grits out.

"Can't I?" I quirk an eyebrow. "Are you sure about that?"

"You're bluffing."

"Do you want to bet on it? You know I never start a game I can't win."

Her face twists in anger, but the moisture in her eyes tells me I got her. She won't tell a soul about Isabelle's secret.

"I hate you," she says before storming down the hallway.

A couple of seconds later, Isabelle stops next to me. "What happened?"

I'm still pissed that Sloane thought she could blackmail me, but I don't want to worry Isabelle.

I force a smile and kiss her cheek. "I reminded her that people in glass houses shouldn't throw stones at someone else's glass roof."

"Did she say anything about knowing you know what?"

"Don't worry about it. She won't tell a soul."

"How do you know?"

"She has more to lose than to gain by revealing who you are."

The deep *V* between Isabelle's brows tells me she's not convinced, so I continue. "Sloane has a dirty secret, one she didn't know I was aware of."

"It seems everyone in this town has secrets."

I rub her cheek with my thumb. "True, but yours is safe."

34

NICOLA / ISABELLE

TWO WEEKS LATER

*S*loane not only keeps her mouth shut, but she also gives Jason and me a wide berth. There aren't any more snide remarks or scathing glances. I decide I don't want to know what secret Jason is holding over her. I have plenty of my own.

Jason and I have become inseparable. There are a lot of practices, and when we don't have school, we spend our time together. I've never felt happier in my life, and sometimes I wonder if this isn't all just a dream.

Jason doesn't talk much about his mother. All I know is that she went back to LA. Good riddance. One less viper to worry about. I'm proud of him for standing up to her. He hasn't talked much about his childhood, but I hope in time, he'll feel comfortable sharing his horrors with me.

I fool myself into believing that I'm not worried about the

recital and the consequences of playing in such a public forum. I know videos of the performance will be posted online, and despite my new nose, darker hair, and lenses, anyone who's heard me play the violin before could recognize me, just like the guy from the music store did.

An hour before the recital, Jason finds me pacing in the empty music room. "What's the matter?"

I give him a tight smile. "Nothing. Just regular jitters. It's been a while."

By the way that he's looking at me, I know he can see through my bullshit.

"Babe, we don't need to go through with it. Say the word and we'll tell Mrs. Simpson we can't perform."

We. Not *you*. This is how far we've come in our relationship.

I shake my head. "I'm fine, Jason. For real."

I look at my reflection in the mirror and smooth the lines of my dress. It's a simple black gown, nothing as fancy as the red dress I wore to his mother's party.

He stops behind me and rests his chin on my shoulder. "You look gorgeous by the way."

I lean into him, and he wraps his arms around my waist. Our gazes lock, and I know this is the moment I've been waiting for.

"I love you," I say.

His eyes widen just a fraction and then he smiles lazily. "I know, babe. I know."

"There you are. I've been looking all over for you," Mrs. Simpson says from the door. "Are you ready? We're about to start."

"Yes, we're ready," I reply.

We follow Mrs. Simpson to the auditorium. There's a separate entrance for the performers, but I spot Sage near the main one, so I tell Jason I'll follow him in a second. I haven't hung out with her in a while, and our texts have been sparse.

"Hey, I'm glad you came," I tell her.

She smiles at me, but she looks sad. "Of course. I'm really excited to see you play. I hear you're wonderful."

"Everyone here is so talented. How have you been?"

"I'm hanging in there. I've been working on a few projects that are seriously kicking my ass."

"What about Eric?"

Her cheeks turn pink. "Are you really going to make me look him up?"

"Yep."

She rolls her eyes. "You're terrible."

I try to stay focused on Sage, but the small hairs on the back of my neck stand on end. I feel like someone is watching me from afar. Dread takes hold of me. I look over my shoulder, but I don't see anyone there.

"Jeez, look at me yapping away." Sage regains my attention. "You probably need to go in, right?"

"Yeah. I'll look for you later."

"Okay, break a leg."

I hurry to the performers' door, but as I'm about to enter, I look toward the main entrance again, where Sage and I were standing a few seconds ago. Then I see him.

Juan.

I couldn't mistake his impeccable blond hair or that arrogant chin anywhere in the world. He glances in my direction, and then he smiles in a chilling way just before he enters the auditorium.

My heart is thumping madly now, and for a moment, I can't draw air into my lungs. The world begins to spin, forcing me to brace my hand against the wall.

He found me. He found me.

The urge to run away hits me, but then I think about Jason and how happy I am here in Triton Cove. Juan already forced me to give up my whole life once. I won't let him do it again. This needs to end now.

I take a couple of steadying breaths, and then pull the door open. I find my place near Jason, and immediately, he senses something is up.

"What's wrong?"

If I tell him Juan is here, he's going to react, but I don't know what he'll do.

I lie, "It's nothing." He's watching me through narrowed eyes, so I add, "You know when you asked me if I wanted to play the solo and I said no?"

"Yes..."

"I changed my mind. I'd like to do it."

"Are you sure?"

"Yes. If you don't mind that I steal the spotlight."

He smiles and then kisses me. "Babe, you can steal the spotlight any time you want."

Mrs. Simpson gives us the signal that we're about to start. We all take our places. The murmur of voices fades away as a pregnant silence drops like a blanket over the audience. An unusual calm settles over my shoulders. I take a deep breath before I rest the violin on my shoulder. We all play together at the start, and then I stand up for my solo.

Jason is sitting across from me. I seek out his gaze and smile. His eyes light up as he grins back. His love for me rolls out in waves, and I use that feeling to reinforce my resolve. Juan thinks he has me cornered. He's going to regret ever coming after me. Our fucked-up story ends tonight.

35

JASON

*I*sabelle's solo takes my breath away. I've seen her perform before, but tonight her flame burns brighter than the sun. The standing ovation that follows confirms it wasn't my imagination. I can't wait to be alone with her tonight to properly congratulate her. For now, I have to stand back and let her bask in her achievement.

There's a reception after the recital, and that's when we need to suck up to parents and alumni to milk them for money. This is a charity event, after all. Isabelle is currently chatting with the Montgomerys, a powerful Triton Cove family. They come to every single event despite the fact that they don't have any children or grandchildren attending the school.

I give the room a cursory glance and spot my mother. My good mood drops to below zero. I was hoping she would skip the recital, but that would be like asking for a miracle. To protect Isabelle from her forked tongue, I walk over before she can ambush us.

The scowl on her face makes it clear this won't be a pleasant conversation.

"Did you enjoy the show, Mother?"

"Oh, yes. I loved seeing how whipped my son is. You disgrace the Petrov line."

I smirk. "Good thing I've always considered myself a Novak."

"Then you really are a fool. You believe the Novaks are gods walking on Earth, untouchable. You'll soon learn you bleed like every mortal."

I don't know if I should consider her statement a threat or simply the ravings of an egomaniac.

"Did you just come here to insult me?" I ask calmly.

"I came to see if there was any hope left for you. I can tell now you're a lost cause."

I roll my eyes, knowing she detests the gesture. "Please, Mother. Why do you have to be so dramatic?"

She laughs without humor. "Oh, you think this is drama? Wait until I take away all your privileges. Who will you be without money?"

I scoff. "Are you threatening to cut me off financially?"

"Yes. I am the trustee of your funds, after all. You can't touch the money your father left you until you're twenty-one." She smiles maliciously, thinking she has me cornered.

It's not the first time she used that trump card to control me, so I was expecting she would go that route. And therefore, I prepared for it.

"Unlike you, I don't need to live surrounded by luxury, and I had one asset that was worth a pretty penny. I think I can survive on sixteen million dollars until I have access to my money."

Her eyebrows rise. "Sixteen *million* dollars? Where the hell did you come up with that amount?"

I shrug. "Oh, I just sold something I didn't need."

The realization of what I did finally dawns on her, making her face twist into something akin to a dragon.

"You sold the Lady Blunt. You had no right."

"On the contrary. I had every right. The Lady Blunt was not part of my inheritance, it was a gift from Grandpa." I smile like a fiend. "You had no control over it."

Fuming, she walks away. I watch her go until she disappears in the crowd. I doubt she'll linger. I begin to retrace my steps toward Isabelle, but Sloane appears out of nowhere and blocks my path. She looks pitiful. Her eye makeup is smudged as if she's been crying.

"Jason, I need to tell you something."

"Jesus, what now?"

Her face is pinched and her gaze is troubled when she replies, "After I discovered Isabelle's secret, I wasn't thinking clearly. I Googled her, which led me to her ex, Juan Alcantara."

My chest feels tight. I curl my hands into fists, but it does little to tamper the rage brewing into explosive levels.

"What have you done?" I ask through clenched teeth.

"I-I wanted to know more about her, so I reached out to him. That was before our conversation."

"You stupid bitch!" I blurt out, not caring that I'm drawing attention.

Her eyes widen and she steps back. "I didn't tell him she was alive. I swear it."

That doesn't matter. It was the clue he was waiting for, and Sloane just handed it to him on a silver platter.

I pass a hand over my face. "Why are you telling me this now?"

"Because I saw him. He's here. I spoke to him... I think he's bad news. He said I wouldn't have to worry about Isabelle any longer."

My blood seems to freeze in my veins. *Isabelle.* He came for her. My pulse is now pounding in my ears as I stalk around Sloane. My mind is focused solely on finding Isabelle and getting her to safety. But there are too many people in my way, and I don't see her anywhere.

The shriek of a fire alarm blares, followed by the fire sprinklers being activated. Chaos ensues. People panic, the women are all worried now about their fucking gowns. I'm past caring about manners. I shove aside whoever is in my path as I search in a panic for Isabelle. I yell her name like a desperate man.

Sage suddenly steps in front of me, her face as white as a sheet of paper. "Jason, you have to help."

"Have you seen Isabelle?" I ask, forgetting to use her fake name.

"Who?" She shakes her head. "I just saw a guy drag Nicola out of the room. She was struggling—I don't think she wanted to go."

I grab her by the shoulders. "Where did he take her?"

"I think he was headed toward the pool." Her expression falls, guilt setting in her gaze. "I should have followed them."

"No, you did well by coming to get me. Find your brother, Finn, and the others, and tell them to meet me there."

"Shouldn't I get an adult?"

I know what's going to happen tonight, and the last thing I need is faculty involved.

"No. Please, Sage, do as I say."

I dash to the first exit I see and then sprint down the hallway, not caring about being subtle. My heart feels like it's going to burst from my chest, and its drumming is louder than my footsteps.

Just before I reach the double doors leading to the pool, I hear Isabelle's scream.

ISABELLE

I TRY to tell Jason that Juan is present, but as soon as the recital is over, we're swarmed by people, and before I know it, we're at the reception and I don't have the chance. I'm trying my best to be polite to the Montgomerys, when in the corner of my eye, I notice Jason walk away.

Shit.

Another minute passes before I manage to excuse myself. I don't find Jason immediately, so I search for the person I must avoid at all costs. Juan.

I spot Sage next to a woman I guess is her mother. I wave in her direction and start toward her. But I barely take two steps before a beefy hand wraps around my arm.

"Hello, cariño. Long time, no see."

Juan smiles seductively, but his steely gray eyes are as cold as ice. It's the gaze of a psychopath. Soulless. My body reacts, seizing in panic. I can't move, and I can't breathe—all I can do is stare at his hateful face.

"What? Aren't you happy to see me?" He traces my jaw with his fingers, sending a shiver of despair down my spine. "Imagine my reaction when I discovered you weren't dead but frolicking away in a beautiful coastal town in California. That wasn't the deal, sweet Isabelle. The deal was for you to be rotting six feet under."

His casual comment about my death snaps something inside of me. I remember who I am, and what I'm fighting for.

"Tough shit, Juan. You can't always get what you want," I grit out.

His nostrils flare, and cold rage shines in his eyes. He tightens his grip around my arm. "You haven't learned your lesson. No one crosses me. I guess I'll have to kill you all over again, and this time, I'll stay to watch you draw your last breath."

He drags me toward the nearest exit. Hell to the fucking no. I open my mouth to call for help when the fire alarm goes off, and everything turns to shit. I still try to break free from him, but his grip doesn't waver.

"Let go of me!" I yell, thrashing against his hold.

No sooner are we in the hallway than he punches me in the face, rendering me useless for a couple of precious seconds. I taste blood, and my ears are ringing. I try to remember my aikido lessons, but it seems I've forgotten everything. Two weeks of practice wasn't enough.

I have no idea where Juan is taking me, because my vision is blurry too. The last time, he took his time using me as his punching bag. I doubt he's going to repeat that again, not when the possibility of discovery is much higher here. Which means I have to escape him before he can kill me.

We go through a set of double doors, and I finally recognize my whereabouts. He brought me to the swimming pool. I see nothing in reach that I can use as a weapon. I pray for a miracle, which happens in the next second. Juan slips on a patch of the wet floor, almost losing his balance. I don't think twice, I body-slam him, and together we fall into the pool.

He releases me, and I don't waste any time. I kick and swim away from him as fast as I can. But my damn long dress tangles with my legs. He catches me and then proceeds to choke the life out of me.

My survival instincts take over. I know I can't dislodge his hands from my neck, but I can inflict pain. I grab his face and press my thumbs over his eyes as hard as I can. Bubbles come out of his mouth as he screams underwater. I'm free again.

I break through the surface with a loud gasp. A coughing fit follows as water comes up my throat. I keep swimming toward the edge, knowing he's right behind me.

"You fucking bitch." He grabs me by the hair and yanks hard.

I scream, but soon it gets muffled by the water entering my mouth when he pushes me under. For a dizzying moment, I see nothing but bubbles of air. I'm drowning, and there's not a damn thing that I can do. I think about Jason, about all the things I didn't say to him, and regret consumes me.

I should have told him I loved him sooner, I should have.... lived longer.

36

JASON

I burst through the doors like a hurricane. The motherfucker is in the pool, too busy drowning Isabelle to notice my presence. I yank my jacket off and dive in. Submerged, I have a clear view of her, and she isn't moving.

No. I can't be too late. I just heard her scream.

My vision becomes tinged in red. I don't care about consequences. I'm killing the son of a bitch tonight. I grab him from behind in a choke hold and yank him away from Isabelle. I'm too aware that I need to end this fast and help her. But it's obvious he won't make it easy for me.

We thrash in the water, and I begin to lose my grip on him. The slack allows him to elbow my stomach, and he breaks free. Isabelle breaches the surface in that moment, and a wave of relief washes over me. But my distraction costs me, and I don't react fast enough to block Juan's punch. My head is thrown back, and blood fills my mouth.

Then there's a sudden pressure around my neck and I'm underwater again. I throw punches and kick him blindly until I connect with flesh. I'm free, but I don't go to the surface. I grab him by the lapels of his jacket and shove him against the wall.

I'm conscious I've been underwater for too long, but I'm riding on my rage. I grab his face and bang his head against the wall again and again. Wisps of blood curl in the water like ribbons, yet I still don't stop.

Isabelle appears next to me, floating like a siren. She touches my arm and pulls me away from Juan. The moment I release him, he sinks, unmoving.

I take a deep breath when I return to the surface, and then I pull her into my arms.

"Are you okay?" I ask.

"Y-yes. How about you?"

"Fine."

I search her face and get hit by another bout of fury when I see the swelling under her right eye. I want to scream and cry.

"I'm so sorry, babe." I kiss her softly on the lips, afraid to hurt her.

"Don't apologize for saving my life," she whispers.

Footsteps echo in the open room. I turn and find Finn, Luke, Reid, and Cameron sporting similar stupefied looks.

"What happened?" Finn asks.

"Isabelle's ex-boyfriend tried to kill her again," I say.

"Isabelle?" Finn raises an eyebrow.

"That's my real name," she replies. "I had to change it and move to Triton Cove because of him. It's a long story."

Luke and Reid walk closer, and then Reid pipes up, "He's dead, isn't he?"

We turn and confirm that most likely, he is.

"Did you…" Finn starts but doesn't finish.

"I have no regrets. He tried to kill us. It was self-defense," I say.

"We need to call my father." Reid pulls his cell phone out.

"No!" Isabelle blurts out. "You can't."

"Why not?" Luke asks.

"No one can know what happened here. If Juan's family finds out we're responsible for his death, they'll come for us, and it won't be pretty."

No one speaks for a couple of beats, but their grim expressions are louder than words.

"I need to get rid of the body," I say.

Finn opens and shuts his mouth. He looks pained, but then he speaks. "Okay. We'll help you."

"I can't let you do that."

"You don't have a choice." Luke steps forward. "I set off the fire alarm. It was in part my fault that Isabelle was taken so easily."

"This is awful. I don't want any of you to be involved in my mess," she replies.

I kiss her cheek, pulling her closer to me. "It'll be okay, babe. Trust me."

"Let's think about practical things," Reid interrupts. "We need to transport the body without anyone seeing it."

"How about we use the laundry cart?" Cameron suggests.

"That's perfect," I say. "Reid, we'll need your SUV."

"No problem. I'll drive around the building and wait for you in the back."

"I'll get the cart," Cameron adds.

"Finn, you probably should be on the lookout and make sure no one comes in here," I tell him.

He nods. "I'm on it."

"I guess I'll help with the body, then. Excellent." Luke smiles like a deranged fuck.

The entire operation takes less than fifteen minutes. Working fast is essential. Thanks to the fire alarm, the school is swarming with cops and firefighters. Thank God the fire

Luke started by "accident" was on the other side of the building.

It's only when we're on the road and far away from the Maverick campus that we discuss how to get rid of the body.

"We should burn it," Luke suggests.

"Of course, you want to set it on fire." Cameron snorts.

"It's the only way to be sure all evidence that could link his death to Jason and Nico—I mean Isabelle—is destroyed," Luke argues.

"But where are we going to burn a body and not draw attention?" she asks.

"I'm glad you brought that up." Luke smiles. "Reid, head to my place."

"You haven't answered the question, Luke." I narrow my eyes.

"I have a furnace."

"What?" Finn blurts out. "Since when?"

He shrugs. "It's new. The guys just finished installing it last week."

"Why do you have a furnace?" Isabelle asks in a wary tone.

"To burn shit, of course. But I'm kind of into working with glass. We'll see how it goes."

"Okay, but how big is the furnace? Aren't they usually small?" Cameron pipes up.

"Please don't tell me we have to chop him up." Isabelle shudders next to me.

"It's big enough to burn a body without turning it into beef stew."

"Thanks for the visual, Luke," Finn complains from the front seat. "That's officially off my menu now."

Isabelle turns to me. "This is truly bizarre. Am I having a nightmare?"

"Considering your ex is dead, I'd classify it as a dream."

I try to guess what she's thinking by staring into her eyes, but they've never been more mysterious to me than they are now.

"Are you okay with all this? I mean, you just killed someone."

I touch her face, cupping it gently. "I rid the world of a monster. I made you safe. I'm more than okay with it. The question is, are you?"

"Oh, Jason. Of course, I am. I'll never forget what you did for me. Never. I love you so damn much."

"I love you too."

"Aww, nothing like a dead asshole to strengthen the bonds of love," Luke jokes.

"Dude, seriously?" Finn complains.

"It's okay. Luke can tease as he pleases." Isabelle rests her cheek against my shoulder and hugs me.

"Don't let this one get away, Jason," Luke replies.

"I won't."

A sense of total peace drops over me. I didn't realize how stressed I was about Isabelle's secret until now. The threat is gone, and I plan to enjoy every day by her side to the fullest for the rest of my life.

37

NICOLA / ISABELLE

*L*uke's house is in a secluded area of Triton Cove and a perfect place to get rid of a body. We could probably bury it in the woods that hug the property and no one would ever find it, but I agree that burning is the best solution.

Maybe I'm still in shock, but I don't feel an ounce of remorse about Juan's fate. He deserved what he got. My only regret is that he didn't suffer more. My neck and face are tender where he choked and punched me, and I'm sure I'll bruise.

Reid parks in the ten-car garage, which is only half filled with expensive cars.

"It seems my mother and Sage are back already."

We texted Sage on the way here to make sure she was okay, and also to stop her from worrying about me. We'll never be able to tell her the truth, though.

We all get out, but when it's time to unload the body, which the guys wrapped in towels, Jason tries to keep me away. "It's best if you don't see this part."

"I already saw you guys fish him out of the pool and load him in the car. I'm not going to break down, Jason. I want to help."

"It's okay, Isabelle. We got it." Luke gives me two thumbs up, smiling from ear to ear.

"Easy for you to say when we're the ones doing all the heavy lifting," Cameron complains.

He and Finn are carrying Juan's body. Meanwhile, Reid is on the phone with someone. He looks serious.

"Where should we take the—" Cameron starts.

"Shh." Reid cuts him off. "Yes, Dad. I'm okay. I'm with the guys. We're all fine." Another pause before he continues. "All right. I'll come home as soon as I can."

He ends the call and then turns to us.

"Is everything okay?" Jason asks.

"Yeah. He was just checking on me because of the fire and all."

"So, no one suspects about…" I look at the body between Finn and Cameron.

"Nope. We're in the clear," Reid replies. "I'm not sure about Luke though. Dad believes it was you who *accidentally* started the fire."

Luke shrugs. "The school can send me the bill for the damages."

"No offense, but this motherfucker is heavy as hell. Can we get going with the plan?" Finn asks.

"Sure. Follow me." Luke spins on his heel and heads toward a door in the back of the garage.

It opens to a path outside. There's a hill and at the end, then another building, smaller than the main house but not *small* by any stretch of the imagination. It's a massive warehouse-type construction.

"Couldn't we have parked closer?" Cameron complains.

"If you're too weak to carry a dead body, then you're not hitting the gym enough," Reid replies.

"Bite me, Bennet."

Luke types in a code on the electronic pad next to the metal door, and then it slides open automatically, revealing a warehouse with workbenches, power tools, and the biggest furnace I've seen in real life.

"Holy crap," Reid blurts out. "You got an industrial one. Is that even allowed in a residential property?"

Luke snorts. "Bitch, please. Everything is allowed when you know who to bribe."

"Don't your parents mind?" I ask.

"My father works a lot and he's never around, and my mother… well, she lives mostly in her own head."

I notice the subtle change in his expression, and that makes me suspect he's downplaying the situation. Guilt pierces my chest. If I were a better friend to Sage, maybe I would know more about her homelife.

"Let's get this shit over with," Jason grumbles.

"Yes, let's," I say.

He looks at me, frowning. "Are you sure you want to be here for this?"

I hold his stare to make sure he reads the truth in my eyes. "Yes. More than sure. I want to see his body burn to ashes."

"Hard core. I like it," Luke pipes up.

There's a thump, and then Finn shouts. "What the hell, Cameron!"

"Sorry. It slipped."

Finn still has his hold on Juan's ankle, so his body is now partially on the ground. The towel covering his face moved, and now I can see his dead eyes and pale complexion. The sight doesn't make me sick though. On the contrary, it brings peace to my chest. My nightmare is finally over, and there's the proof.

Jason strides toward them and shoves Cameron out of the way. "Just go help Luke with the furnace."

"Help how? It's already on."

"Yeah, it takes days to get them hot enough to melt shit. You can't really turn them on and off all the time," Luke explains.

Reid covers Juan's face again, and then Jason lifts him up. His white shirt is still damp, highlighting his flexing muscles. My body heats up, and the butterflies in my stomach come to life. I'm getting turned on by watching my boyfriend dispose of my evil ex's body. God help me.

Jason seems focused on the task, but then he looks at me and smirks. He knows my mind is in the gutter. It's probably written all over my face that I want to screw his brains out when this is over.

Luke is waiting next to the furnace, and the heavy metal lid is open. I can feel the blaze from where I stand. I don't know how he can manage to be so close to the furnace without an ounce of discomfort.

"Should we just toss him in?" Finn asks Jason.

"Yeah. Let's swing first to gain momentum. On the count of three. One…two…three!"

Juan's body flies into the furnace, and the orange hue coming from it becomes brighter.

"Oh my God. Burning flesh stench. Close that damn thing, Luke!" Cameron covers his face with his shirt.

"What? You never ate roasted pig before?" Luke asks innocently, but at least he does shut the furnace.

I get closer and stop next to Jason to peer through the small opening. I meant what I said earlier. I want to see him turn to ashes. Jason throws his arm over my shoulders and pulls me closer. I lean into him, resting my head against his frame. One would think we're staring at the sunset.

"So…" Luke starts. "This will take two to three hours. Anyone want to come to the house to grab something to eat?"

"Seriously? You're thinking about food now?" Reid asks.

"Uh, I could eat," Finn replies.

"Me too," Cameron adds.

"What about the lovebirds?" Luke glances at us.

Jason looks at me first. "What do you want to do, babe?"

I could stay here for the whole three hours, but if I say so, Jason will stay with me. He's been through hell, and he needs a break from all this morbid stuff.

"Sure, let's eat," I reply.

"Cool." Luke claps his hands together. "Don't worry, Isabelle. That piece of shit isn't going anywhere."

"Unless he's a demon, but then, we're all fucked." Cameron laughs.

"You're an idiot, Cam." Finn shakes his head.

We let the guys walk ahead of us. Once we're inside the main house, Jason stops and waits until they disappear down a long hallway.

Then he leans in and whispers in my ear, "Can I show you something first?"

His warm breath against my skin makes me shiver. "Sure."

He links his fingers with mine and steers me in the opposite direction. We pass several grandiose rooms, and soon I realize this is not a mansion, it's a fucking palace. I'd easily get lost here.

Finally, he stops in front of a set of double doors and pushes one open. The room is dark, but the moment we step inside, the lights turn on. They aren't bright, just strong enough to reveal a wicked-cool display room. There are so many pieces of art that I don't know what to look at first.

"Wow," I say. "What's all this?"

"Luke's father's collection. These are all props from famous movies."

"Oh, so not expensive art?"

"I'd say everything here is expensive."

He takes me to the center of the room where a vintage town car has the prime spot.

My eyes bug out. "Is that the car from the *Titanic* scene?"

Jason chuckles. "Yep. Come on. Let's get inside."

He opens the door for me, and I slide into the back seat. I expect Jason to get behind the steering wheel, but he joins me in the back.

"I didn't know you were a fan of the movie?"

"Never watched it."

"Then what are we doing here?" I ask, but one glance at his smoldering eyes, and I have my answer.

He reaches for my hair, tucking a strand behind my ear. "I've always wanted to fuck in this car."

The simmering desire turns into a volcano, consuming my entire being.

"Well, then put your hands on me, Jason."

"I'll put everything on you. My hands, my mouth, my cock."

He kisses me hard while he runs his hand down my dress.

"I prefer your cock *in* me," I reply against his lips.

His fingers find my pussy and I moan out loud. "I know, babe. But you like my fingers there too, right?"

I bite his lower lip in answer, and then I get busy getting rid of his shirt. I want it gone. I'm too impatient and end up popping some of the buttons.

Jason laughs. "Eager, aren't you?"

"You have no idea."

"Confess. You were checking me out at the warehouse."

"You know I was." I pepper his jaw and neck with kisses, and then I run my tongue over his chest.

Jason grabs a fistful of my hair and yanks at the strands. The sting of pain sends another zing of pleasure down my back and straight to my core. He keeps fucking me with his fingers, and when he presses his thumb over my clit, I shatter into a million pieces.

"Oh my God, Jason."

"That's right, babe. Say my name."

I capture his face between my hands and kiss him again, deep and hard, before I pull back. "I want to ride you."

"Damn straight you will."

He makes quick work of his pants and boxers, and like a nympho, I straddle him, impaling myself on his cock. Jason grabs my hips and helps with the pace. The car begins to rock from side to side, the old suspensions squeaking loudly, and the windows fog, just like in the movie. Our mouths are fused together again, as if we both want to meld into each other.

I've never wanted anyone as ferociously as I want him. I've never loved anyone more fiercely either. He's everything to me, and that's a thought that should scare me, but it has the opposite effect. I've never felt more serene, more certain of myself in my entire life.

"Isabelle, Isabelle. You drive me wild, babe. I'm so close," he rasps against my lips.

"Fuck me harder then."

The noise we're making is almost deafening, and there's a high chance we'll damage the car, but we're both past caring. My orgasm is approaching fast, my toes are curling inside my shoes, and it feels like I'm spinning out of control. When the tremors hit me, I scream against his lips. He grunts a couple of seconds after me, but we don't stop moving until much, much later. I climax again before we stop completely, and I rest my forehead against his shoulder.

"Holy shit," I blurt out.

"You can say that again. That was... I have no words." He kisses me on the cheek.

Someone whistles from outside, and it echoes loudly in the room.

"Shit. We've got company," Jason grumbles.

"Luke?" I ask him softly.

"I hope you guys are done with post-murder sex. Pizza is ready."

Jason chuckles, shaking his head. "No. Surprisingly, that was Finn."

38

JASON

TEN MONTHS LATER

I wake to the sound of the ocean, and it feels like I'm still dreaming. Isabelle snuggles against me, pressing her nose against my shoulder. My arm is wrapped around her waist, and her leg is covering mine.

"Good morning, babe." I kiss her forehead.

"Is it morning already?"

"I'm afraid so."

There's a knock on the door, and then Isabelle's mother asks if we're up already.

I say, "Yes," at the same time Isabelle says, "No."

"You'd better get going or you'll miss all the fun," Carol Maldonaro singsongs.

"Tell me again why we agreed to go with them to explore the town at this ungodly hour?" Isabelle asks.

I chuckle. "I was trying to score brownie points with your folks. I don't know why *you* agreed."

After graduation, Isabelle and I decided to take a trip, and the first stop was to visit her parents in Costa Rica. They'd made enough money in their careers as executives for big international corporations to be able to retire early. Their beachfront house in Santa Teresa is a little piece of paradise, and I wouldn't mind staying for a while.

We had to tell them about Juan's visit to Triton Cove, which gave me plenty of anxiety. I didn't want them to look at me and see another monster. But they treated me like a hero and made me feel like I was part of their family already. I've never experienced anything like that in my life, and I'm still pinching myself, thinking this is all a dream.

For all intents and purposes, Isabelle is still Nicola Devlin, because resurrecting Isabelle would be too suspicious. She hasn't decided yet if she'll return to the music scene as a new prodigy. For now, she's happy to travel and play with me. And I've been busy composing music, which it turns out, is what my passion truly is.

As far as we know, Juan's family doesn't suspect we're responsible for his disappearance. This we learned from her parents' lawyer in Spain, who helped them fake her death in the first place. It seems the asshole never told anyone what he was up to, and he might have used fake travel documents to come to the US. He was careful to not leave any trail that could link him to Isabelle's death if he had succeeded and, in the end, that worked in our favor.

"I only agreed because you seemed keen." She hits my chest playfully.

"Well, I am, actually."

She leans on her elbows and stares into my eyes. "Are you going to finally step out of the shade and get some sun? I'm beginning to think I'm dating Edward Cullen."

"Well, your name *is* Isabelle. Maybe I *am* a sparkling vampire."

"Hmmm, are you going to bite me, then?"

I roll on top of her, pressing my morning wood against her pelvis. She wiggles underneath me.

"I know what you're doing." I caress her face, still mesmerized that she lets me worship her after our rough beginning.

Her beautiful violet eyes widen innocently. "I have no idea what you mean."

She parts her legs, and my cock slides to her entrance. Damn it, she's so wet that it wouldn't take much to sheathe myself in her.

"We don't have time," I say.

Smiling like a little minx, she wraps her legs around my hips. "I say we do."

I kiss her deeply as I plunge into her heat. The bed creaks as I move, making her giggle.

"God, I hope your parents are eating breakfast on the patio outside," I whisper against her lips.

"Stop talking about them."

She captures my lower lip in a love bite. The sting sends a zing of pleasure all the way down to my balls. I try to move at a steady pace to minimize the noise, but hell, I can't go slow when the reward is so sweet and just around the corner. I pump in and out faster, and it's like a damn orchestra is in the room. Isabelle becomes tighter around me a second before she gasps loudly. I cover her mouth with my hand, groaning a moment later as I come.

There's a sudden, loud *crack*, and then the whole bed collapses with a terrible bang. I stop moving at once and ask, "Are you okay?"

"Yeah. So much for not making too much noise."

I slide off her and sit up. "Shit. I can't believe we broke the bed."

To my surprise, Isabelle starts to laugh hysterically.

"This isn't funny. What are your parents going to think?"

She's laughing so hard, she's crying already. "They'll think you're a sex machine."

I run my fingers through my hair. "Great."

"Jason, babe. It's okay." She touches my arm.

I try to scowl, but I can't when she looks so happy that it makes my heart overflow with the same emotion. I crack a smile. "If they say anything, I'll blame you."

"That's fine."

My phone rings, making me frown. I got a new number specifically for this trip because I didn't want to be bothered by anyone—a.k.a. my mother. Only Finn and Luke have this number, but they were instructed to not call unless it was an emergency.

Isabelle, knowing this, looks worried. "What do you think happened?"

I jump to my feet. "Only one way to find out."

I fish the phone from my backpack. "It's Finn," I tell her.

"Answer it already."

"Hello?"

"Jason, I fucked up," he says in a freaked-out voice.

"What happened?"

"I… I hurt someone."

My heart twists painfully in my chest. "How? Please tell me not on purpose."

Finn is the nicest guy I know—I'm certain he wouldn't hurt anyone deliberately, but he's a Novak, and it seems our family is cursed.

"No, but it doesn't matter." His voice breaks. "He's just a kid and… God, Jason, it was awful. I need you. Please come home."

I lock gazes with Isabelle. She must have overheard part of the conversation, because her eyes are filled with distress.

"I'll be on the next flight out. Don't worry, Finn. We'll sort everything out."

When I end the call, my heart is as heavy as lead. Isabelle is already on her feet, collecting our things.

"You don't need to come, babe."

She whips her face to mine. "Finn is in trouble. Don't expect me to stay behind."

"What about your parents?"

"They'll understand. Family is everything to us."

"That's my point. You haven't seen them in a long time. I won't be upset if you don't come with me."

Her eyebrows arch. "You misunderstood me. Finn is family to me."

When I didn't think I could love this girl more, she proves me wrong.

I reach her in a single stride and pull her against me. "I don't know what I did to deserve you."

"Everything, babe. You did everything, and I'm yours for as long as you want me."

"Then be prepared for forever."

*** THE END ***

Thank you for reading *Falling for Catastrophe*. I hope you enjoyed Jason & Isabelle's love story. If you did, please consider leaving a review.

Curious about what happened to Finn? Read his story in *FLIRTING WITH DISASTER, already available.*

ONE-CLICK NOW!

How can you crave someone as intensely as you hate them?
Finn Novak is one of the young gods who rule this town and wreaks havoc wherever he goes. He's above everything, even the law.
I never thought I'd be thrust into his world of depraved privilege until tragedy strikes, and I'm forced to attend Maverick Prep, his domain.
I vow to keep hating him but quickly become trapped by his web of twisted mind games. I yearn for his barbed words as much as I hunger for his touch.
Getting close to Finn means unveiling secrets that should stay hidden. But like bodies buried in shallow graves, skeletons never remain in the closet forever.
I can't escape him, though. His darkness feeds mine, and it's only a matter of time before the void consumes us both.
When the story is over, who will be revealed as the real monster? Finn or me?

ONE-CLICK NOW!

FREE NOVELLA

CATCH YOU

Want to read another enemies-to-lovers sports romance? Then **scan the QR code** to get your free copy of *Catch You*.

Pride and Prejudice meets Veronica Mars in this enemy-to-lovers romance.

Kimberly

I had always thought Owen Whitfield fit the mold of the

brainless jock perfectly. Group of idiot friends? Check. Vapid girlfriend? Check. Ego bigger than the moon? Check. As long as he stayed out of my way, coexisting with his kind was doable. Until one day our worlds collided, changing everything. He pissed me off so badly that I had no choice but to give him a taste of his own medicine. Little did I know that my act of revenge would come back to bite me in the ass. How was I supposed to know Owen would turn out to be the best partner in crime I could hope for?

Owen

I never paid much attention to Kimberly Dawson, but I knew who she was. Ice Queen was what we called her. She was gorgeous, no one could deny that. But she was also a condescending bitch, which was enough reason for me to stay the hell away from her. She thought I was a dumb jock, and that was okay until she came crashing into my life. Against my better judgment, I let her embroil me in her shenanigans, forcing us to spend too much time together. It was my doom. She got under my skin. She was all I could think about. I never thought I would be the knight in shining armor to anyone, not until she came along.

Scan the QR code to get your FREE copy!

ABOUT THE AUTHOR

USA Today Bestselling Author Michelle Hercules always knew creative arts were her calling but not in a million years did she think she would become an author. With a background in fashion design she thought she would follow that path. But one day, out of the blue, she had an idea for a book. One page turned into ten pages, ten pages turned into a hundred, and before she knew it, her first novel, The Prophecy of Arcadia, was born.

Michelle Hercules resides in Florida with her husband and daughter. She is currently working on the *Blueblood Vampires* series and the *Filthy Gods* series.

Sign-up for Michelle Hercules' Newsletter:

Join Michelle Hercules' Readers Group:
https://www.facebook.com/groups/mhsoars

Connect with Michelle Hercules:
www.michellehercules.com
books@mhsoars.com

- facebook.com/michelleherculesauthor
- instagram.com/michelleherculesauthor
- amazon.com/Michelle-Hercules/e/B075652M8M
- bookbub.com/authors/michelle-hercules
- tiktok.com/@michelleherculesauthor?
- patreon.com/michellehercules